One Night at Finn's

A Finn's Pub Romance

R.G. ALEXANDER

One Night at Finn's
Copyright © 2017 R.G. Alexander

Formatted by IRONHORSE Formatting

ISBN: 1977986927
ISBN-13: 978-1977986924

Dedication

For all my readers and Finn Club friends who go all in,
thank you for your unwavering support.
And to Cookie - Love is the reason.

CHAPTER ONE

The Dry Spell Diaries
by JD Green

Dear Diary,

Confession time.

When I first agreed to publically document the arid Sahara that is my sex life, I had a few reservations. A few reservations, a few manly panic attacks, a few dozen arguments with my editor... But despite initial concerns, I promised to climb out of my hermit's cave and go on a date or two, sharing the details in this diary for your amusement and edification.

I freely admit I was hoping to get something out of it in return. Based on the title, I think everyone knew what

I wanted that something to be.

It rhymes with trucking.

I never imagined I would still be in this dry spell six months in. All men love trucking, right? Even more unbelievable is the fact that I'm starting to seriously think about giving up my search in favor of commitment instead.

That's right. I used the C word. Not one of my old favorites like cock, copulation, concupiscent or cum. Commitment.

I've never been against it, but it wasn't what these diaries were supposed to be about. Yet, here we are. I think I'm finally ready to start a long-term, monogamous relationship.

I might even be in love.

Sure, it's with an Irish pub...but the heart wants what the heart wants.

pauses respectfully for the incoming deluge of side eye

It's not exactly a lie. Hot men and cold beer make Green a happy boy. And Finn's Pub has both in spades.

Longtime readers know about my macro obsession with microbrews and the man candy attached to this place via blood and marriage. Add a friendly LGBT atmosphere and some great local music? If this pub were a man I'd already be picking out cock rings.

With so much going for it, Finn's should at least be— if not my inanimate soul mate—my perfect destination for romance. And by romance I mean mutual attraction that inevitably leads to… We're all adults here, right? Can I stop saying trucking now?

Too bad that's not in the cards tonight. At least, not with the guy I'm loosely calling my date.

The drought continues.

Nothing to see here but stilted conversation mixed with excruciating silences. I'm writing this during one of the many lulls so you can appreciate how bad it is in real time.

I can take a lot, but I'm not sure I'll make it through this night without crying Uncle. Think I'm exaggerating? In the last hour, I've been considering worse forms of torture to make myself feel better.

*I've gone through everything from having my balls slowly nibbled off by schools of carnivorous goldfish, to being trapped on a twelve-hour flight beside some nose-picking troglodyte underlining his fifth copy of **(Blah) Racist Political Assertion (Blah)** to pass the time.*

Good book title. If it's not already taken, I'll write it

in my spare time. All the spare time I won't be spending having sex. Ever again.

Three strikes, T. You're a dear friend and there's nothing I love more than watching that Australian drama about women in prison with you snuggled up on Mr. Lumpy. (My couch, you perverts.) But sadly, you know nothing about what stirs this gay man's soul.

Want to hazard a guess as to which soul I'm referring to? Yep. The one in my pants.

Which brings me back to the guy who will never *get in my pants. I won't name names, but his mullet wants me to call him Billy Ray. He is the last straw on the giant haystack in the barn of my matchmaking failures.*

I went too far with that metaphor.

I'm done being set up. It never ends well. Sometimes it never ends at all. Seriously, has it only been three hours? If this night goes on much longer it might throw me into voluntary celibacy for the next seven years. In Tibet.

And now I'm thinking about Brad Pitt. You know, because he was in that movie Seven Years in...never mind.

Am I a magnet for the creepers of the world? Do you people look at me and think, "I've got a cousin who still

4

lives with his mother and hasn't clipped his toenails in five years because he wants to be Wolverine. Oh and he's gay, so I bet he and Green would hit it off."

It takes more than dick to make that *my type.*

That word might be the crux of my problem. Maybe no one can find me a match because I don't think I'm an actual type myself. Unless None and/or All of the Above is an option.

I don't know why it's such a difficult question for me to answer. But because it is, I've decided to put it to you. If you had to choose, what type do you *think I am?*

Call it a challenge. I'll share some stats and you *can tell me what you think. Unless you believe—as I secretly do on days like today—that types are a fallacy concocted by the same charlatans who sold us Valentine's Day and pheromone cologne? You'll give it a shot. Think of it as contributing to a worthy cause.*

The Get Green Laid Foundation. Donate early and often.

Game on.

I'm a six-foot, twenty-six-year old man who's been blessed with a fast metabolism and some decent muscle mass, which is good since at heart I'm a couch potato that lives in flannel pajama bottoms and stocks ice cream—Moose Tracks please—and bottles of barbecue sauce in my kitchen at all times in case of an emergency craving or the apocalypse.

I don't usually eat them together, and I never expected Armageddon until this last election cycle, but I've always been prepared. Just in case.

I read science fiction, gay erotic romance, historical biographies and wilderness survival guides—my foster brother, Stewart, writes those, and I consider that a necessary evil, since quoting his books to him verbatim gets me out of his annual camping trip.

In my defense, I love nature. What I don't like is the idea of my brother forcing me to start fires with two sticks and a ball of my own hair. Not to mention all his hopefully unrecorded TED talks about urine.

Did you know that urine is basically the coconut oil of survivalists? Good for everything from tanning leather to dyeing fabric? You could even distill it to make potable water if you were desperate and dehydrated enough. I'm not saying you should gargle that shit or use it to condition your hair—notice I said I'm *not saying that. But at some point I'm afraid Stewart might, and then I'd have to ship him to the nuthouse and change my number. That could make for awkward family reunions.*

Moving on.

I was raised in Washington—think Seattle not DC—but I spent my college years braving the deep red heart of Texas and dating a closeted cowboy before deciding to try the East Coast on for size.

Everything about me is literally all over the map.

Try filling out that *online questionnaire. Or at least, try to do it without getting matched with a lily-livered cowpoke that dumps you for a rodeo queen the night of your graduation.* After *receiving a life-altering blowjob from yours truly.*

Yeehaw.

Tale of woe aside, my dry spell isn't voluntary. I didn't make a vow of celibacy as an act of self-flagellation in remembrance of that dill-hole Rod. It just happened. Or didn't happen. And then it didn't happen some more. In fact, it's been not happening for so long I'm worried it might be a permanent condition.

Unfortunately for me, pickings are slim and our city's infamous Finn clan is running out of family members…

***

"That is so hot," My date says, startling me back to

the present. "You text faster than anyone I've ever seen."

"Thanks?" A texting compliment? That's a first. Though it's the fiftieth time he's used the word *hot* in a sentence. I email my unfinished article to myself for later, and offer an apology. "Sorry about that. When I get an idea I tend to—"

"Whatever," he interrupts impatiently. "I told you I'm not interested in sharing life histories. I'm not here to talk. Not that we could hear each other in this wannabe hipster dive if we were."

Unfortunately, I can hear him just fine. Also, since I've been told more than once that my reading glasses, my hair and the usual tightness of my jeans are all the height of hipster fashion, I should probably be insulted for all the wannabes of the world. In case I am one.

"I'm surprised you don't like it. Finn's is an institution with two generations worth of local history. You grew up around here, didn't you?"

He glances down at his phone distractedly.

Does he think he's being subtle? That I can't hear the game he's been playing on that thing all night? He didn't even bother to turn down the volume.

"It was better before the old man gave it to his kid," he finally responds. "Not as crowded. Now there's never a good seat, the music blows and they don't serve anything decent. We should have stayed at your place."

That was never on the menu. I'm about to say so out loud when his hand cups my knee under the table and squeezes suggestively. His fingers are freezing and I notice at the same time that his upper lip is sweating. Why is he so nervous?

"Why don't we get out of here while we still can? Find something else for you to do with your mouth."

"Excuse me?" I no longer feel sorry for him. At all.

"When Toni told me how hard up you were, I thought this might be a pity fuck. But you look like you could be a model or something with all that girly hair and those big brown eyes. I've had half a chub all night. You're really hot."

The romance. Make it stop. At least use a different adjective.

"Toni didn't tell me that much about you." She'd skipped important descriptors like *sleaze ball* and *jackass* and *never-in-a-million-years*.

"She wouldn't," he snorts. "But you'll find out all you need to know as soon as we get somewhere I can unzip in private. You ready?"

And I've officially had enough. I would dump my

9

drink in his overheated lap and say something clever, but I'm not big on scenes, he's not worth the wit and my beer is gone. I opt for walking away instead.

I stand, keeping a tight grip on my empty mug so I don't "accidently" fling it in his direction. "I'm staying. I've got friends at the bar I need to say hello to. But I get it if *you'd* rather call it a night."

He studies my glowering face for a full thirty seconds, then sighs and goes back to playing on his phone. "No, that's fine. We have time for one more drink."

We have time? I'm not sure how long it'll take him to figure out his time is up, but I have no fucks left to give. This date is over.

I'm still muttering to myself about dense pricks with bad haircuts when the crowd parts and I see what might be a mirage. The kind that makes me instantly forget about the Billy Rays of the world, and has my mental iPod rocking a medley of songs about hot, sweaty sex.

I wouldn't be surprised if the three men I'm hallucinating were waiting to receive individual keys to the city for improving the view and increasing tourism. I subtly glance around for a cameraman. Maybe this is a new marketing campaign for the pub?

Unable to resist lingering for a moment of silent appreciation, I swiftly take in the redheaded giant and the lean, longhaired temptation at his side. But my attention stutters and stalls when I get to the older man in the trio.

Did I say man? My mistake. I'll be damned if that's not Big Daddy Zeus himself.

I think I found my type.

I volunteer as tribute. Or born again virgin sacrifice. Does Zeus like virgins? What about younger men who are ready, willing and able to worship at his shrine?

Or bend over and call him daddy. Whatever he's into. I'm easy.

What you are is a sick little freak, Green.

If having to subtly adjust myself in public as my inner voice slut shames me doesn't make me turn away, I'm not sure anything could. Something about him demands my attention. A pull I can feel from across the room, a hard tug from the pit of my stomach.

Lower.

Lust at first sight is a new experience for me, and I'm not sure I like the sensation. I definitely don't understand it. Why him? The bar has been full of eye candy for hours and I've reacted the way I always do. Observe, appreciate and move on. But I can't move on this time. I'm stuck and every molecule in my body is pointing at this one specific man like a dog catching a scent.

It doesn't make sense.

He "smells" unattainable. Unattainable is your jam. Remember Chad? Remember Roddy?

Those are unfair comparisons. My reaction to Zeus leaves my high school crush *and* my last rodeo clown in the dust. My first blowjob, the one that blew the lid off my head and confirmed my sexuality, comes closer to what I'm experiencing now. But I have a feeling it's only the tip of this potentially filthy iceberg.

Filthy is the right word for all the things I'd like Zeus to do to me.

There's a distinct possibility that he's out of my league and I'm not tall enough to ride his rollercoaster. But just because I've never experienced anything like it doesn't mean I don't want it as badly as Jack secretly wanted Rose to scoot over and share her flotation device at the end of *Titanic*. Because of course he did, and I can't believe people are still arguing about that twenty years later.

On any other day I'd be making a list of all the reasons I'm right about that, but Zeus is attempting a casual lean I don't want to miss. It's not very successful, since even in faded jeans and a clinging, navy blue t-shirt, there's nothing casual about him. His posture is too good, for one thing. There's steel in his spine. Unbending. Resilient.

This is crazy. The way he *stands* is turning me on. Maybe it's the out-of-place awkwardness of it. It makes him seem less like a figment. It also tells me he doesn't seek out bars like this very often. The weekend crush is too rowdy and crowded for a guy like him.

He's used to being in control. I'm only guessing, but it must be true since I have the strangest urge to salute him…then take off all my clothes for a thorough inspection.

Military? Cop? BDSM Dom? I'd bet money this man is in charge of something involving orders and uniforms. Maybe handcuffs, but that's not a given and I'm not that lucky.

I try to focus on specific features to get my mind out of the gutter, so I start from the top. His hair is short and dark and even from here I can see silver sprinkled liberally at his temples and laced through the full trimmed beard that makes him look like a Clan Chieftain or a sexy Greek fisherman. I think I'd like to feel that salt and pepper scruff rubbing against my skin.

These fantasies are writing themselves.

Zeus isn't as tall as the ginger tank beside him—maybe a few inches taller than me—but he's still rippling with muscle and imposing in a way that screams contained power and good genes. Nature built that edifice.

I have the urge to move closer and take in more details. I need to know what color his eyes are and what he sounds like when he speaks. But instead I'm rooted to the floor, wondering how I could have gone twenty-six years without experiencing this kind of life-altering ache.

I want him. Now. Yesterday. In the parking lot. On my knees beside the dumpster. Bent over in a bathroom stall. I swore I'd never be that guy, but for him I think I'd be willing to go there.

You don't know him.

No. I don't.

I may hand out romantic advice for a living, but secretly I'd always assumed that the instant spark people talked about was bullshit. It's never happened to me, and I see hot men all the time. I've dated some, ogled others. I'm friendly with a photographer that regularly emails me pictures of nude male models for inspiration. Sometimes they're fans of my column and ask him to pass on their numbers.

I love looking at them, and my body reacts to the visual stimulation, but I've never been compelled to call or meet them in person. Instead, I take pieces of my favorites and mentally paste them together for a private session later. My regular Franken-fantasy has the UPS guy's forearms, my old English professor's hair and Wolfgang from *Sense8*'s self-confident penchant for nudity. The rest of the scenario is usually made up of rotating porn gifs and my vivid imagination. It works.

But I don't think that's going to cut it anymore. Not after today.

The intensity of my physical reaction to Zeus is causing me concern. Is it hot in here? Is my blood pressure rising? Can a person stroke out from excessive arousal?

Obviously it can kill brain cells, because I'm tempted to walk across the bar, take this unknown element by the hand and beg him do things to me. Rough things. *Filthy* things.

This is not me. I'm the easygoing, good time guy. The nerdy gay sidekick in the PG rom-com of your choice. I don't do violent passion for bearded strangers, and I'm not about to go up and introduce myself and— I'm already on a *date*, for God's sake.

I *was* on a date. But Billy Ray might not know it's over yet and he's still in the building. There has to be a rule. Like not swimming for thirty minutes after you've eaten. *Don't proposition a guy at a bar when the loser who just propositioned you is still sitting at your table.*

I give Zeus one last defiant glance to test myself. Instant fail. Instead I'm swallowing a whimper as his stern expression transforms into a smile.

Because his smile is glorious.

But it's not for me. He's watching the giant wrap his fist around the slender man's braid to bring him in for a kiss.

My mental iPod offers up an impressive record scratch when I finally realize exactly who he's standing with.

Why the hell is my Zeus with a Finn?

He starts to turn his head in my direction and, before we can make eye contact, I find the willpower to look away. I force my feet to move again, wondering at my odd reluctance to let him out of my sight. This is ridiculous. *I'm* ridiculous. The probability that he's straight or—with the stories I've heard about the Finns and their proclivities—ménage bound, is too high for me to be this much of a mess. *Ménage.* The thought is both arousing and soul crushing at the same time.

Either way, if he's with them he's not for me. He's not out of my league, he's in a different solar system. I need to be a grownup and move the fuck on.

"Fiona," I call as I set my glass down with more force than necessary. "Emergency refill. Brady Stout. Stat."

"Another pint of BS for JD, ASAP."

The old men on the corner stools laugh and the sound buoys my spirits. When Seamus Finn turned half of this place into a microbrewery, he'd taken to naming his creations after members of his own family. Everyone was still getting a kick out of the clever gimmick.

My favorite, the stout, was christened for his cousin—aka the kissing ginger with possible dibs on Zeus. It's a thick, Guinness-like offering that goes perfectly with my mood, as well as the chorus of drunken singers trying and failing to keep up with the energetic Irish band.

I could live at this bar. I wasn't exaggerating that much when I said I was in love. The drinks are good, the mood is lively and I always get a warm welcome from the regulars. It makes me wish I drank more, so I'd have an excuse to linger and listen to their stories. Sometimes you *do* want to go where everybody knows your name.

I bet a lot of people secretly think of the old sitcom *Cheers* when they find a bar they like. I can't be the only one.

The one thing that could make this moment better is the absence of the guy at my old table. Or Zeus deciding to take his place. Because he's gay and he knows I exist.

#DreamonGreen

I will.

Fiona tilts her chin in my date's direction. "When are you going to bounce the bozo, JD? You've looked miserable all night, and I already lost my bet on how long you'd last thirty minutes ago."

Fiona and I audited a class together a few semesters ago and the two of us just clicked. Partly because we're both the kind of people who graduate from college—me with a double major and her with a master's degree in psychology—but keep compulsively returning like educationally starved junkies. And, yes, partly because she mentioned she worked here and it was a good excuse to visit while researching the same things she claims to on a nightly basis.

Observing men in their natural habitat is our secondary obsession. A truly good bartender and a man who gives relationship advice for a living need to do a lot of research. It's all very innocent, you understand. *For work.*

"I already did my bouncing. Sort of," I finish glumly, since the bouncing would be more effective if he actually went away.

"You don't sound too sure." A good-looking man with wavy blond hair and pretty blue eyes sends Fiona a grin over my head, joining the conversation. "How does a guy *sort of* end a date?"

"Don't tease him, Wyatt. JD is a gentleman, and gentlemen have a hard time ditching their dates just because sex is off the table. Pay attention now. You might learn something."

"Are you saying I'm—you mean the brunette last week?" His expression instantly transforms into offended with a side of panic. "Fi, a guy at the firehouse set us up, but we didn't spark so she decided to go home alone. *In a car that I paid for.* I *didn't* ditch her and *I am* a gentleman."

That was...adamant.

"You don't have to convince us, firecracker," Fiona scoffed, shooting me a look that tells me this is their normal banter and she's enjoying it. "But we're talking about someone else's sex life today, not yours. You're being too nice again, aren't you, Green? I can always tell."

"No I'm not. I told him he could leave if he wanted to and I glared. *A lot*. It's not my fault he didn't catch on. He probably still thinks we're hooking up tonight."

"You glared?" She laughs in delight. "God, you're so cute. I dated a Canadian like you once. Dirty and creative but *unbelievably* polite. Some men, however, are dickheads that need a more obvious kick to the curb."

Maybe so, but if growing up with nine other boys taught me anything, it was when to pick my battles. And when to hide in the attic with a good book until they forgot I existed.

I *am* still upset that he didn't think he had to do anything tonight but show up. That he assumed he'd get laid because we were both breathing and in the same room. But it's not like I haven't experienced it before.

Guys like that—straight, gay or in between—think getting off is the point so dating is a waste of time. Why put in the effort to wine and dine a talking glory hole?

To a Billy Ray type of man, I'm the happy meal after choosing the drive-thru. The movie he watches online so he doesn't have to put on pants and leave the house.

The age of instant gratification is making everyone too damn lazy. Especially when it comes to romance. Nobody works for anything anymore. Nobody pays attention to the details.

I check on my mullet man, notice he hasn't moved at all, and turn back with an eye roll for my audience. "I'll start the curb kicking after this drink, if it's all the same to you. I've got time and he isn't bothering anyone. I think he's still working on his high score at Candy Crush."

Wyatt choked on the beer he'd been swallowing. "Wait. He's been playing a game on his phone *during* your date? And he still expects to get laid?"

He stands while he's speaking and I notice how lean and muscular he is. And there's a tattoo on his biceps that makes it clear he's a fireman and proud of it. Nice.

Why can't Toni hook me up with a guy like this?

"Idiots like that give the rest of us a bad name. Hold my beer, folks. I'll be right back."

My eyes go wide, and Fiona watches my expression

transform while she pulls her multi-hued hair back into a ponytail.

"What is he doing?" I whisper, equal parts horrified and enthralled.

She grins at me. "Taking out the trash, hon. Finns are good about that kind of thing."

Wyatt is a Finn too?

I should have known. All the good ones in town are taken, straight, or belong to that family. I wonder where Zeus fits in?

Stop thinking about him fitting into something. Watch the show instead.

"He can't throw someone out for being a shitty conversationalist."

"Hell yes he can. And the boss would back him up if he were here. Even the more commitment-phobic members of their clan have certain behavioral standards. And they're all overprotective of their family and friends."

My confusion must be easy to read because Fiona kindly covers my hand with hers. "You're *my* friend, JD, and this guy wasn't treating you with the respect you deserve. I've been watching your face all night, so don't deny it. That's all Wyatt needed to know to do the right thing." Something flashes in her eyes as she watches him tap Billy Ray on the shoulder, her tongue poking out to fiddle with her lip piercing thoughtfully. "It's sweet, really."

It is. Sweet and unexpected. And after less than a minute of whispered conversation, my so-called date is tossing a few bills on the table, grabbing his phone and disappearing out the door.

He didn't look for me once.

Insulting? Probably, but I feel more relieved than anything. Sure, I'll need a ride home later, but that ride won't smell like cheese or have cold, wandering hands.

Bonus.

I hear Fiona telling two servers nearby to take over before she leans her elbows on the bar. "Why are you still frowning? This is good. You're now free to join me in a study of all things Irish and male. Too bad you were sick for St. Patrick's Day. We could have written a paper on the copious alcohol consumption, kissing and booty pinching that occurs each year to celebrate a religious zealot with a snake phobia."

"A snake isn't always a snake."

She wrinkles her nose. "And a cigar is never just a cigar. In my professional opinion, Freud can suck it."

"Who can suck *what* now?" Wyatt slides back into his seat with a shit-eating grin.

"Cigars and snakes and shitty dates. We're speaking in phallic symbols," I explain, lifting my glass in his direction. "And on that note... Hail the conquering hero. As handsome as he is noble and brave."

"It was nothing. Really. No big deal at all." Wyatt's smile wobbles and he hunches his shoulders, getting that uncomfortable look I've only seen on heterosexual males when gay men give them compliments. It's funny, but I still feel sorry for him when Fiona laughs at his expense. He did do me a giant favor.

"That wasn't a come on, I swear. All it means is your next drink is on me. And thank you."

"No drinks. I mean, you're welcome, of course. And I'll drink, but you don't have to *buy me* a drink. Not that you couldn't if you wanted to, but I get a discount anyway so…"

"Poor Wyatt," Fiona croons as he stammers. "His family of big, strong, strapping homosexuals has traumatized him. He thinks being gay is contagious."

"If only." Did I say that out loud? Apparently, because they both start chuckling, and I watch the fireman's shoulders relax again, along with his smile.

Good.

Wyatt nudges me apologetically with his elbow. "You know I don't really think that, right, JD? Fi likes to pick on me, but I'm man enough to admit that you're a handsome guy. If I swung that way, I'd be on *all that* in a heartbeat." He waves his hand toward my face and body. "Unfortunately, I've only got eyes for this one bartender I'm trying to wear down."

I'm getting that loud and clear. I'm also getting that Fiona is keeping Wyatt at a friendly distance, which is strange since she usually goes after what she wants. I'd wonder about it, but when she puts another drink in front of me—did I already finish that last one?—I realize that this is not the night for me to pry. She knows what she's doing. Probably.

"To the ever-stout Brady," I say instead. "Thick, potent and the only thing I'll be swallowing tonight."

Wyatt spits his drink across the bar and onto Fiona's chest, but before I can tease him about it, the beer's namesake arrives and starts patting him helpfully on the back.

My embarrassment is close to crippling as my gaze travels up a thick tree trunk of an arm to monster biceps and a set of shoulders Atlas would envy. Crap, what is it

25

with me and the mythological references tonight?

"I'm already spoken for," Brady Finn says with a friendly smile. "But I'll assume you're talking about your beer."

"Never assume, big guy." This from the boyfriend. He appears right beside Brady with a wicked curve on his lips. "You *are* thick. And potent. But I'm the only one who gets a taste."

"You're making him blush," a new voice observes quietly.

No.

He can't be here. I was good and resisted temptation. I walked away. When I glance up to verify his presence, the blush he's referring to blazes hotter across my cheeks.

Zeus.

And I'm dead. I'll just sit here and hope the floor opens to swallow me up soon. Or they all disappear. Whichever comes first.

CHAPTER TWO

Two gay icons, a Greek god and a firefighter walk up to me in a bar…

The start of an epically dirty joke? No, this is really happening. I'm wide-awake and Zeus is within touching distance.

This couldn't possibly go horribly wrong and end in tears.

Wyatt is still apologizing to Fiona and trying to "wipe" his beer off her breasts, but she pushes his mischievous hands away and smiles up at my hallucinations. "Hey Brady. Ken. I thought you'd be tied to the dart board all night."

"I'd rather tie him to things in private," Ken winks at her. "But he promised Owen we'd come out for a drink, so here we are."

Brady sends his fiancé a heated look before lifting his massive shoulders in agitation. "That *was* the plan, but I'm not sure why we bothered. He sent a text five minutes ago. He and Jeremy decided to stay home. Said he didn't think we'd mind since we already had company."

What kind of company? Just friends company? Ménage company?

"They're staying home again?" Wyatt sounds so disappointed it distracts me from my Zeus obsession. Maybe it's the journalism major in me. You know how people are always saying they wished they'd been a fly on the wall for these kinds of conversations? There are Finns at Finn's pub discussing Finn things right in front of me. I'm finally the fly.

That sounded more impressive in my head.

"They're acting like an old married couple again."

"They *are* an old married couple, idiot."

Wyatt shakes his head in irritation. "Not *that* old. We haven't hung out with him in months. You'd think they'd want to come up for air occasionally. Hell, you'd think Owen had never had sex until they got together, and we all know that's not true. The guy was with a

28

different woman every night."

But he married a man, you sweet summer child.

I bite my cheek to keep from smiling when Fiona appears to be thinking along the same lines. "You've never had truly great sex before, have you, Wyatt?"

His glare is defensive. "All I'm saying is when you make plans with family you should keep them." He looks down at his knuckles and I hear him muttering to himself. "Never had...yeah, right...I'll show *you* great sex..."

This is *so much better* than my date.

Ken shares a look with Zeus before nodding in my direction. "Who do we have here, Fiona?"

"We have here a Mr. JD Green. He's a good friend of mine who needs our help recovering from a bad date."

"*Fiona.*" Why would she say that in front of them? In front of *him*?

The ginger decides to take pity on me and holds out his hand. "Nice to meet you, JD. I'm Brady Finn and this is my fiancé, Ken Tanaka."

"I know," I tell him, after waiting a beat for him to introduce his company. He doesn't, and it's frustrating enough to make me forget myself. "Nice to drink you."

Shit.

"Nice to *meet* you," I repeat, setting my mug down carefully. "I should slow down with this recovery plan of Fiona's. My filter is gone."

This is the lie I tell in social settings to make people feel better about talking to a crazy person. I've never had a filter. I was born with a full head of hair, a birthmark shaped like a half-eaten slice of pizza on my hip, and shitty conversational skills.

Ken laughs and slips his arm through Brady's. Unconscious possession, I note absently. No jealousy, just pride and the kind of love that hurts to look at. "Where did you two meet?"

Fiona swiftly hails my brilliance, mentions the courses we've taken together and the fact that I work online without going into specifics. But when she starts to describe this evening's crash and burn episode, or at least, what she observed of the disaster? "Not cool, friend."

I think our next togetherness class needs to be Etiquette 101.

"I'm getting you a second opinion, *friend*. You need to stop letting your neighbor find your dates. That girl has horrible taste in men."

She doesn't know the half of it. Toni moved next

door to me four months ago, after her abusive ex had beaten her for what she'd decided was the last time.

I knew her from work. She does the sales and marketing for the LGBT e-zine I write for, and we'd shared email on a weekly basis and lunch once a month or so for editorial meetings. That was our only connection until that night.

When she'd reached out for help, I was the one who answered the phone. I put her up on my couch, helped her get in touch with my landlord and loaned her enough pocket change to get the basic essentials until payday.

It's not as big a deal as Toni makes it out to be, but she's wanted to do something for me ever since, which is how I ended up in this situation. Maybe I could convince her to bake something instead. Teach me to crochet. Anything.

"She's fired," I swear. "Though the winners she's been picking have definitely made the series more popular. Maybe she's a mole for my editor. If I'm laid and happy, my dry spell will end and he might lose ad revenue." I tsk and shake my head. "This is really his fault when you think about it. We should TP his house for being a cock blocker."

"I don't think I'd go that far, hon."

Ken's jaw drops while Fiona is talking and I realize I over-shared. I quickly look away, only to find myself snared by the black gaze of Zeus.

Dark coffee. Rich, potent espresso. I'd wondered what color his eyes were and now I know. I also know his lashes are thick and black, his laugh lines are deep and expressive, and once again I'm mesmerized.

It's like staring at the sun.

There's a herculean effort to resist my urges going on inside me. The ones that want me to climb his beefy body like a jungle gym and nibble on his neck while he takes me right here against the bar.

Did I mention it's been a while?

Ken taps my shoulder and I flinch in surprise, but at least it distracts me from my more depraved impulses. "You're *that* JD Green? *Go For Green*? We read you all the time."

"You're a writer?" Zeus reveals that rasping voice again, the one that makes my balls tingle. Does he gargle with broken glass and whiskey? And do I detect a barely there southern drawl? Despite my bad experience with Rod, a southern accent is still one of my weaknesses. When this man speaks, I instantly think of front porch swings and carriage rides and our bare-assed, sweaty bodies slipping against each other in the heat.

He asked if you were a writer. Stop staring and answer. I nod dumbly, finally tearing my gaze from his and turning back to Fiona.

"Cut me off," I demand dramatically. "My secret identity has been compromised."

"Sorry about that." *Liar.* She isn't sorry at all. She isn't even trying not to laugh.

"Isn't *Go For Green* what Tasha's been reading at the dinner table lately? The Finn Fan Club guy?"

"There's no fan club," I tell Wyatt quickly.

At least, I don't think there is.

But if there were it would be my fault and I'd be the president.

Yes, okay, I mention their names in my column every once in a while. Who wouldn't? They made being gay in this city look good. Marriage, kids, sexy billionaires… The Finns are basically the Kennedys of the neighborhood. A family full of gorgeous Irish overachievers that keep hooking up with equally impressive and newsworthy partners.

The latest love match was the best so far, since it included my favorite YouTube personality, Essie Mills. Well, her brother, I guess. But he works with her so he's cool by association.

The point is, they were local legends *before* they started coming to the dark side. Now that they have, they're more popular than ever.

If you lived in Metropolis, would you *not* want to read about the way Superman fills out his tights or what he likes to do on his nights off?

I rest my case.

Ken turns toward the man that still hasn't been introduced. "JD writes a relationship advice column. The Dry Spell Diaries are a more recent addition where he goes on dates—specifically bad ones—and writes it down for our enjoyment. We never miss an entry."

Zeus is still watching me as he takes that in. "So the man you were with tonight was for work."

"You could say that." Putting it that way makes me feel like less of a loser...but a little more like a male prostitute.

Fiona chuckles. "I like the way you think, buddy. Just for that, your next beer is on me."

"I wasn't expecting it to become a regular feature," I explain stiltedly, feeling his attention like a physical caress on my skin. "And believe me, I'm not agreeing to bad dates on purpose. It's hell on my brand. Who wants romance tips from a guy that keeps striking out?"

"It's relatable," Brady assures me. "Everyone knows you give good advice, but that doesn't mean you automatically get a happy ending for yourself. And from the comment section, your readers love it."

"People respect honesty." The wisdom of Zeus again.

Okay, I can't keep calling him Zeus. Not if he's going to be talking to me and staring at me *as well as* starring in all my future sex dreams.

"People like to slow down for car wrecks too, which is why my love life is so popular. Have you noticed we haven't been introduced yet?"

His eyes widen and I take that as a no. "You know my name, but I don't know yours, or anything else about you."

"Oh, this should be interesting." I hear Fiona murmur to Wyatt. "Tell us about him, JD. Do your thing and tell us who *you* think he is."

I don't need to be asked twice. I lean an elbow on the bar and study him as if I'm trying to solve a mystery. "You don't have blue eyes, so odds are low on you being a stray Finn family member. Plus, these two referred to you as *company*, which implies friendship instead of blood relation. Since Ken is relaxed around you but

Brady is deferent, I imagine you were either a peer he respected or his superior at some point. You're also both practically standing at attention in the middle of a bar on a weekend. I'm cheating a little because I know Brady's work resume, but which initials are we talking about? PD or USMC?"

That's me being subtle.

And *maybe* showing off.

Brady eyes me with admiration and pats Zeus on the shoulder. "That is a scary party trick, Green. Master Sergeant Willis was my senior drill instructor at boot camp. This man got me through some rough times and into the best shape of my life. And he only made me cry twice."

He said that like it was a compliment. With a straight face.

"What a sweetheart," I mutter, flushing when I see his lips curve in amusement.

"No one has ever called me *that* before."

Poor Zeus. I can fix that for you. "I still haven't gotten your first name. If this keeps up I'll think you're a spy."

"Carter." That husky rasp sends physical vibrations up my spine. "My name is Carter. And if I *were* a spy,

I'm guessing your skills would have caught me out by now."

Master Sergeant Carter Willis.

A Marine no less.

Woof.

He's younger than I first assumed. Early forties, at most. That touch of silver in his hair is sexy in an Anderson Cooper kind of way. Only Cooper doesn't have a beard or look like he could chew nails for lunch and survive a hostile alien environment without backup.

He's so damn—what's the word I'm looking for? Masculine? Alpha? Sexy as fuck with a ninety-nine percent probability of being off the market and/or hetero?

This perfect specimen from the land of testosterone is also a walking recruitment poster. Just looking at him gives me the urge to do more with my life. Be all I can be. Maybe take up wrestling.

Now I'm imagining the two of us wrestling.

Spoiler Alert: I'm naked and I let him win.

He's still staring. With a slow blink he scans me from my lucky red Chucks to my blue and grey flannel, his eyes narrowing on the t-shirt beneath that reads, *Speak Friend and Enter* in Elvish. A nod to my level of geek.

I'm suddenly insecure about my choice of casually mismatched dating attire. Should I have worn a suit and tie to the pub? The mauve, silk poet shirt I got for Christmas as a joke from one of my brothers?

I've never been into false advertising. I am what I am, and sadly, it isn't Popeye. More like a hybrid of Olive Oil and Wimpy, if we're telling truths. For those who aren't in the know, picture flailing limbs and a perpetual case of the munchies.

No wonder I can't get laid.

But from Carter's expression, he likes what he sees. Does he know what he's doing with those eyes of his? I'm either drunk enough to be delusional, or this drill instructor is giving me the look. The, *I'm interested in wrestling with you naked* look.

I might have been thrown off by his rugged looks, age and military background, but I honestly can't tell which way he's leaning. He hasn't gotten weird around Brady and Ken, but all that means is he's a decent guy. Is it possible he's actually—

You're delusional, Green. You have to be. Abort. Abort.

Brady's head swivels back and forth between us, and I realize my ogling has gone on long enough for the others to notice. It might be time for me to leave before I embarrass myself more than I already have.

"Nice to meet you, Brady. Ken. Gunny." I scoot off my stool.

Brady snorts at that. "What? I watch movies," I mumble. "What's the damage, Fiona? Since my date has officially bailed, I think it's time for Cinderfella to head home and finish that diary entry."

I reach into my pocket for my wallet and scroll through the apps on my phone for a ride, picking my poison as I pay my tab.

"No way," Fiona protests, holding my card like it's her hostage. "We finally got you to ourselves and you're leaving?"

Wyatt slings a friendly arm over my shoulder. "He's not going anywhere. Once Seamus finds out you were in the pub, he'll flip. As in, he'll be jealous I'm here and he's not. No one's been jealous of me in years. Not since my calendar days. Don't take this away from me, man."

I feel a wide smile form at his earnest request. He's clearly the goofy puppy of the family. And he's bonded to Fiona, so what she wants, he wants too. "I shouldn't."

I *really* shouldn't. My attraction to Carter is a neon sign pointing to probable humiliation and inescapable sexual frustration. It would probably surprise my readers if they knew how inept I truly am at social interaction. That's one of the reasons I write about sex and relationships more than I participate.

JD gets high marks for observation. Participation? Not recommended.

"You should," Ken insists, guiding me over to a nearby table before I can resist. "And we're covering your tab. It isn't every day we get a chance to hang out with a local celebrity."

"Says the high-tech genius engaged to the senator's ex-body man." I snort and collapse into a chair closest to the wall, thinking about how strange this night is turning out to be.

Tanaka's smile is sharp and curious. "You've got us over a barrel, Green. You know all about us—excluding Carter, of course—but we don't know enough about you. Except now I can say you look younger than I thought you would, and you're almost as pretty as Brady's brother, Rory."

He and I both know he could change that information imbalance in less than three minutes with his smartphone. With his skills he'd know what color underwear I'm wearing, and I swear *I* can't even remember what I put on at this point.

"He's got nicer hair," Wyatt offers up generously. "And he's nowhere near as arrogant."

"Who would be with his history?" Brady teases. "There's another thing we know. You have shit taste in men and you can't get laid to save your life. But that's not exactly a state secret, is it?"

I don't respond to the gentle jab because Carter chooses that moment to sit down beside me, close enough for me to feel the warmth radiating from his body. The heat he's giving off burns my skin and I press my hand to my cheek. Maybe I'm coming down with something.

"Until recently, you weren't exactly known for picking winners yourself." Is Carter defending me? But Brady doesn't seem to mind, nodding agreeably before slipping an arm around his fiancé.

"I had a nice long dry spell because of it too, so I can relate."

Ken whispers something in Brady's ear that has the ginger's chest rumbling with subdued laughter. Then he glances over at me again. "Speak, friend. Tell us your secrets."

My secret is I'm wondering what Ken's boyfriend

would say if he knew that the only man I could imagine *tasting* right now is the one he admires. The mentor of masculinity that made him cry.

The one who is scooting his chair right up against mine until I'm trapped between his furnace of a body and the wall. Is he trying to block my escape?

Like I'd want to get away.

"I'm an open book." And that higher pitch I'm speaking in must have something to do with the combination of tight pants and a full erection. Hopefully it doesn't cause lasting damage. I cough and lower my voice. "An overly wordy technical manual, really. One you only read when you're trying to find a cure for insomnia."

His soft chuckle has me shifting in my chair. "Doubt that."

Two words and I'm hot butter. Melted. Spreadable.

I meet his gaze. "That I'm boring? Believe me, it's true. Ask the guy who left less than an hour ago."

Carter stops smiling.

What did I say?

"Don't listen to JD," Fiona says, shattering the tension. "He's overly cautious and too nice as a rule, but I would never call him boring. That guy was an ass."

"Always trust Fiona's judgment about people. So sayeth Seamus." Brady's grin widens as he takes in Carter's seating arrangements. "If she tells us your work date was an ass, we believe her, right Carter?"

"Ask me. I saw it first hand, and the ass was strong with that one." Wyatt sets down a fresh beer for himself and straddles a chair on Carter's other side, leaning around him to catch my eye. "All right then, open book. How does a not-boring, overly cautious single guy with your dating record decide to become an advice columnist? Tell us everything."

Big mistake, asking someone like me to do something like that. Especially when I'm desperate to distract myself from my reaction to Carter Willis.

Because I totally do. I tell them everything.

***

I wander through the empty parking lot hours later, waiting for my ride and chuckling at my own expense.

JD Green closed down a bar. What a wild one. And—stop the presses—he had a great time with a table full of interesting, attractive men. And one Fiona.

It's still hard to believe that reality surpassed the gossip about the Finns. At least, it did if those two are anything to go by. Brady is practically a saint, and Wyatt's a big talker with an almost obstinate naiveté, but a mushy, gooey center. They were funny, smart, personable... And the way they talk about their family with so much devotion? Who wouldn't admire that? Imagine being part of it?

Speaking of things I'll be imagining *for the rest of my life*... Carter was the best date I've had in years.

He wasn't your date.

Semantics. Parts were touching, drinks were shared and ideas exchanged. In the fan fiction of my life, it was definitely a date.

He was quiet, but I don't think it was because he's shy or lacking in opinions. The man had a very expressive face, if you were paying attention. But he seemed content to listen to the conversation flowing around him, to let it wash over him while he observed.

He was observing you. Listening to you.

It was refreshing. Strange. A little suspicious.

I'm not used to anyone listening like they're filing away my answers. Like what I'm saying matters.

It never has before. Full disclosure? Half the things I say are bullshit, the rest are answers to Trivial Pursuit: The Hollywood Edition. But he made me feel like I was revealing buried treasure when I told them how I'd harnessed my inability to stay out of other people's business into a viable career. How I double majored in journalism and psychology. Why I turned down a more prestigious magazine's offer to write for a local online publication instead.

He was interested in every word. And there were so many of them. My only excuse for talking so much is that his nearness drove me insane.

That and the constant touching. His leg against mine. His arm brushing my back or my side each time he shifted in his seat. Nothing I could point to as confirmation of flirting, but the possibility alone made sitting beside him feel like the world's kinkiest foreplay.

I still don't know that much about him. All I found out could fit into a frustratingly small beer glass. Originally from North Carolina, he'd chosen to retire after several decades in the service and he'd recently moved to town to work with Ken and Brady.

And he smelled like the woods. Fresh and clean and irresistible.

I can't remember being attracted to an older man before, no matter how good he smelled. He'd been a Marine as long as I've been alive, so he has to have at least sixteen years on me, but my dick doesn't seem to mind. It wants to see him again as soon as possible. So do I.

Not that I'll get another chance. Somewhere between our exhausted bartender closing up and my last trip to the restroom, I lost sight of him before I could get his number.

That was my plan. What new guy in town would turn down a friendly digit exchange? It's always good to have someone on your speed dial that can point you toward the best restaurant or most reliable dry cleaner. Someone you could call if you woke up in the middle of the night with the need to talk. Or, you know, have passionate, explosive sex.

I thought I was frustrated before, but it's nothing compared to this. The need feels different now. Stronger. And it's no longer a random itch anyone can scratch. Now it's all about Carter.

"Finally."

What the fuck? "What are you doing here? I thought you left hours ago."

Instead of answering, Billy Ray surprises me with a chokehold that cuts off my air and drags me back to the side of the building. Fuck, he's stronger than he looks.

"You got him?"

"Yeah," Billy Ray grunts at the stranger as I struggle against him. "I thought he was never coming out. Probably had a few more dates to line up. Fucking fag."

Fucking fag? This from the guy who kept asking me to blow him? Panic sends spikes of adrenaline through my veins and I lodge my elbow as hard as I can into his gut. That frees me, but only long enough for the unknown assailant to pin me against the wall.

"If you'd gone in to get him like I told you, it wouldn't have been a problem." He taps my cheek in a fast, stinging slap. "Stop squirming so I can talk to you, Green. You like to talk, don't you? Got a way with words? I know you've been the one badmouthing me and convincing her not to come home. Did you really think I wouldn't get her back?"

It takes me a minute to register his words. Her? Home?

The switch flips and suddenly I know who this skinhead-looking asshole is.

Toni's ex. He's talking about Toni.

"Fuck off and leave her alone," I snarl defiantly, pushing against him. "She doesn't want to have anything to do with you."

Asshole responds with a laugh and a sucker punch that shocks all the air from my lungs.

"Yeah, you'd like to think that. You're not getting any, so nobody else gets to either, is that it? I know all about your little diary. Shit, the only reason I let her keep that job was because you were a bunch of harmless dick lovers and the money was good. But that's over now. As soon as we have a chat about you staying out of my business, I'll be giving her all the dick she can handle."

She took him back? Did he force her? Did he make her set me up with his friend so he could—

I can't think anymore as the two men start to *chat*. One fist glances off my cheekbone while another, less forceful punch pounds into my side. It still hurts like hell, but I'm counting my blessings that they're either almost as bad at fighting as I am, or not really trying to kill me. I dodge as much as I can, swear and kick out, managing to connect with someone's thigh. I hear an agonized shout as my left eye swells.

"You queer piece of shit," Billy Ray whines. "You almost kicked me in the *balls*."

"I can't kick what you don't have, jackass," I manage. I'm hoping the driver I called will show up soon to scare them off. Until then, I'll have to distract them.

"Come closer and I'll give you what you begged me for a few hours ago." I mime jerking off with my hand, baring my teeth in a grin that's all bravado.

"I didn't want that." I hear his quick denial, followed by a push that slams me back into the wall. "It was an act. You were the one begging for it."

"I'll never be that desperate." There's blood in my mouth and I grimace at the coppery taste. "A waste of closeted space and a guy who has to hit girls to make his tiny prick pay attention? I wouldn't touch either one of you if you paid me."

The tiny prick in question bunches my shirt in his fist, tightening the fabric around my neck. "Shut your dick-sucking hole or we'll forget we're just talking and get serious."

But I can't. I refuse to go down like this. To let an eighties' reject and his abusive buddy beat me up outside a bar. It's too fucking clichéd.

"I'm guessing you're the dick-sucker," I challenge Asshole. "You should know your buddy wants it bad. He was practically pushing me out the door, desperate to get some before you got here." I try to laugh, but cough

49

instead when his fist twists, tightening the fabric like a noose. "You two are perfect for each other."

I might have gone too far. *No filter* is not a noble cause of death. I see the rage building in Asshole's eyes and I'm really wishing Fiona hadn't parked out back. That big, intimidating Brady was still here. That I could—

"Who the hell are *you*?" Asshole asks before he releases my shirt, disappears and let's out a scream that's loud enough to wake the dead.

I slouch against the wall and rub my sore throat, trying to breathe. Why is he making so much fucking noise?

I hear talking over the rush of blood pumping through my veins and then Toni's ex is whimpering. "You don't need to call the cops, man. I'll go. Please. It hurts..."

Am I a bad person for enjoying that? My knees go liquid, my back scraping down the bricks until my ass hits hard concrete. I hear myself moan, but it's more from relief than pain. I'm just happy my part in the punching and choking portion of the evening has ended.

"*Damn it*." The curse is followed by swiftly retreating footsteps.

I think it's over. And I might need to throw up.

A pair of large, calloused hands push the hair away from my face, and when I try to jerk away instinctively, they freeze. "They're gone, JD. It's Carter. Carter Willis. You're safe, but I need to make sure it's okay to move you."

I let out a shaky breath. "Carter. Good. Safe is good. But I'm not in a hurry to move anything."

Safe is good.

"Can you open your eyes?"

"Of course I can." But do I want to? Not at all. "What are you doing here?"

There's silence for a heartbeat or two, and then, "I was trying to stop you from getting your ass kicked. You want to tell me what *you* were doing out here alone in the first place?"

That gets me to open my good eye and glare. *Really?* "I'll give you a hint. It wasn't ballroom dancing."

"I guessed that much on my own," he grits, studying my injuries. "Can you stand?"

Before I manage a response his arms slip around me, and he's carrying me as if I weigh nothing. I'm not sure if I'm impressed or completely emasculated.

"I can walk," I offer politely through stiff lips, leaning my heavy head on his shoulder to soak in his strength.

I don't think I'm lying. I could walk. But this is nice too.

"Did you get a good look at them?" The question pierces the fog I'm drifting in. "I only saw the one, but I'm hoping you can describe them in more detail to the police."

"Of course," I mumble into his neck, inhaling his woodsy aroma distractedly. "It was Billy Ray and Asshole."

Strong arms tightened around me. "You *know* them?"

"Asshole is my neighbor's ex-boyfriend. The other guy was my date."

Carter is swearing under his breath until we reach a brand new, shiny black truck. "Brady was right after all," he says finally, managing to unlock the passenger side door while balancing me on one knee. "You have shit taste in men."

And you can't get laid to save your life.

Tell me about it.

CHAPTER THREE

I lived in Texas. That fact keeps rattling around my battered brainpan as I sit in the passenger seat beside Carter and watch him white-knuckle his steering wheel.

I had fast, forbidden and sadly unsatisfying sex with a closet case—*in Texas*—and I'd never been harassed or beaten by any gay-bashing stereotypes before.

It happened here. In a liberal city, at a gay friendly bar, with a man I'd let pick me up at my home. The unexpected nature of the attack somehow makes it worse.

Growing up with Rick and Matilda—foster parents who'd given me nothing but total acceptance since I was four—I'd thankfully missed the prayerful reprogramming, physical bullying and verbal abuse that too many people I know had to suffer through when they came out to their friends and family.

Matilda had taken me out for new sneakers and a haircut, handing me a giant bag of chocolate kisses that I'd munched on throughout the day until my stomach ached. She said her mother had done the same when she'd gotten her period, and it was the only rite of passage she knew. Over dinner, Rick took his turn at being supportive in his own unique way, listing off every important figure in history that also happened to be gay. Then he quizzed my brothers and me to make sure we'd been paying attention.

I was lucky.

I'm *still* lucky.

Logically, I know they didn't attack me because of my sexuality. That was all about me getting between a victim and her abuser. The fact that I was gay just conveniently allowed them to trick me into a date in order to get me somewhere alone for our *chat*. It didn't make what happened any less disturbing.

"Fag." Punch. "Queer." Punch.

I don't like the way I'm feeling after that. I'm not talking about the physical discomfort, though I won't lie. Everything hurts right now. What I hate is that they made me feel vulnerable. Weak.

But the text I got from Toni as we left the police station was much worse.

I'm sorry.

She knew. She somehow knew what happened, what they'd done, and all she had to say was *sorry*?

Tomorrow I'd try to be more understanding. I'd remember all the psychology classes I'd taken and realize she probably didn't believe she had a choice. She'd spent years being someone else's punching bag, and he'd convinced her that was all she was. All she was allowed to be.

But tonight a woman I'd still been defending as I filled out a report on my two attackers left me to be beaten in the parking lot of a bar. One text can't make up for that.

"I should take you to the hospital."

I glance over at my scowling savior. "I'm not doing the suffering in silence thing," I promise, even though I kind of am. "That one cop with EMT training felt me up. He says, and I'm quoting here, that I'm *damn lucky*. He also swears nothing is broken, I'm probably not bleeding internally and I'll most likely feel better tomorrow. I'd rather not spend hours in the ER waiting for them to tell me the same thing with a higher price tag."

"A cop felt you up?"

That was all he got from that? I would laugh if I weren't worried I'd dislodge a rib. "He had a hairy mole on his cheek," I tell him with mock-solemnity. "I was too distracted by it to resist."

A vein in his temple throbs, so I don't think I made him feel any better.

All I want to do is cuddle up to a few dozen icepacks and go to bed. But there's no way I'm going back to my apartment tonight, and I should probably tell him before we go too far out of his way. "Could you drop me off at the Hyatt around the corner? Just turn left at the next stopli—"

"No."

"No?" I repeat dumbly. "Why not? Don't tell me it got a bad Yelp review."

He glances over at me, gaze narrowed. "Because of your neighbor? Is that why you're not going home?"

So he'd been listening when I gave my statement. "You could say that."

You could also say that I'm not emotionally ready to face the aftermath of misplaced trust. That I don't have the energy or strength to defend myself if she isn't alone and push comes to more shoving. But "because of my neighbor" is less wordy, so we'll stick with that.

Room service also sounds like a plan worth sticking to. Pay-per-view, ice machines and those decorative soaps that are too small to do any good if hygiene is an actual concern. I'm sure that's all the medicine I need. A little chicken soup for the spoiled man's soul and I'll be able to face the repercussions of my life choices in the morning.

Pausing at the light, Carter blows out a forceful breath and then yanks on the wheel, doing a U-turn on the abandoned street. "You're coming home with me. You can sleep in my guest room."

"What?" I reached up to gingerly cup my jaw after jerking it in his direction. "*Ow.* No I'm not. I mean, *thank you*. For everything. I don't know many strangers that would spend the whole night looking after a guy who let two idiots get the drop on him. You don't need to do any more."

"I let them get away."

"You saved my ass, Carter. I heard what you said to the cops. When I collapsed, you let go of Tweedledumbass to check on me and they both bolted. But the end result is all that matters. I'm still standing.

You're still standing. The heroes win and truth and justice prevail."

He lifts one shoulder to shrug off my words. "I wasn't paying attention. I was talking to Wyatt and I let you..." He trailed off, expression grim with self-recrimination. "I didn't realize you were standing out front alone until Fiona told me."

My chuckle comes out sounding more like a ragged hiss. "It hasn't been anyone else's job to take care of me for years. But don't worry, this is not something I plan to let happen again. Defense classes are in my future. Maybe Kung Fu. I'll find someone to call me grasshopper and start wandering the West promoting peace with my mad skills. I'm not shaving my head though. Wyatt said he likes my hair."

He's fighting a smile. I can tell. "As we prize peace and quiet above victory, there is a simple and preferred method. Run away."

If my jaw weren't swollen it would drop to my knees. "Holy shit, Carter. Did you just quote *Kung Fu* to me?" Did a drill instructor, a *Marine*, just quote a fictional Shaolin monk from a seventies television show?

Now is not the time for me to get turned on. *That's not sexy. That's not sexy.*

That is *so fucking sexy*.

And that thought right there is why I shouldn't be going home with him. Not for a reason like this, anyway. An injured, helpless, not sexually motivated reason. I need to think of something else, but the options are dwindling with every mile. "I could call Fiona."

She wouldn't say no. But we haven't been the kind of friends that ask for more than notes from class and a sympathetic ear now and then. Thinking about it now, I don't really have any, *"let me stay at your place while I recover from a beating"* sort of buddies. Especially since Toni is no longer an option. Just study groups, work friends and online fan forums.

I should fix that.

My new friendship goals don't help me tonight, and the idea of Carter taking me to his place has me feeling guilty, embarrassed and yes, pathetically turned on. I'm sore, not dead.

"Fiona must be asleep by now. I'm not and I have the room."

He's acting like this isn't a big deal, but going home with someone I met in a bar isn't my usual MO. It's not that I don't think I'd be safe with him. A career Marine. A friend of the sainted Brady.

59

The man I've wanted to do filthy things to all night.

But I usually deal with my problems on my own. I like taking care of myself. I always have.

So stop being a wuss and go home.

I can't. Not tonight.

"It's late, Green," Carter continues. "You and I know what the best move is here. You'll stay with me and we'll both get some sleep."

He sounds tired, and I feel guilty. He did save me. It would be rude to say no.

Don't do it. Don't use that lame, "it would be rude" excuse.

I lean my head back and let my shoulders relax as I ignore my doubts and give in to the inevitable. I might as well, since he doesn't seem to be willing to look at other options and I'm in no shape to argue. "I appreciate the offer."

His sigh sounds relieved. "Thank you."

I only wanted to shut my eyes for a few seconds, but when I open them again we're already pulling into a driveway. His driveway. And the two-story house at the end of it looks like it belongs to a family of five. "This is your place?"

Well damn. Am I about to meet the wife of Zeus?

That would be the only thing that could make this night complete. A jealous Hera punishing me for daring to think about her husband's ass.

He turns off the ignition with a nod. "I'm renting it from Tanaka. He has a few houses in the neighborhood and this one was sitting empty. Too much space for only me, but I'm grateful. It's going to take a while to get used to the quiet."

I think about my busy apartment complex and the dorm before that, not to mention my crowded house growing up. I get where he's coming from.

Carter has been in the military for most of his life. That's not an environment conducive to elbowroom. After living like that for so long, you either crave silence, or you need noise and distraction and can't sleep without the lights and the television on.

Helpful hint: choose your channel wisely. Dreams can get weird if you fall asleep during a *Sharknado* marathon.

"This *is* a lot of space for one guy. I don't feel as bad about borrowing your guest room now."

"You shouldn't." He gets out, coming around swiftly to open my door and help me to my feet. "Most of the second floor is a gym, but there's one bedroom with a full bath up there, plus two guest rooms downstairs, so you can take your pick once we get you cleaned up."

Did he say we? "I don't know if I care about a shower as much as I do an available pillow."

Not entirely true, because a large part of me needs to wash this experience away. But the louder voice is begging to be knocked unconscious for a while. To stop the wheels from spinning in my brain, worrying about things and people I can't save or change.

Carter puts a sturdy arm around my waist and guides me up the walk, using his key and opening the front door with his free hand. "I wouldn't be a good host if I didn't make sure you were clean and fed and I at least checked your injuries. It won't take long."

I feel small beside him, though he only tops me by two inches. I think it's more about what he exudes. *Strong. Steady. Safe.* I'm reacting to it, even though I know I shouldn't be.

When I said I could take care of myself I meant it. I've been slapping on Band-Aids and cooking my own frozen dinners since I was old enough to reach the microwave.

Matilda was a first class cheerleader for personal freedom and a lioness if the cause was just, but if she'd ever stepped foot in the kitchen it was after I left for college. She was too busy working as a civil rights attorney and saving the world. She didn't have time to stop and bake us cookies.

I could use the lioness right about now. And a cookie.

I take in as much as I can with my one good eye. Large foyer. Open kitchen and living room design, both of them individually bigger than my apartment. Both basically absent any decoration. Understandable, since he just moved in. Carter turns right down a hall and walks me through a bedroom. This must be his.

Jesus, that bed is enormous, I think, as he leads me to the master bath. Orgy-enormous. Harem-enormous. Does he have a harem hiding somewhere nearby?

"This place came furnished, but my room has the best shower," he mutters out an explanation, making me wonder if I was thinking out loud again. "And the towels and first aid kit are here."

He places a thick blue towel by the sink. "If you think you can clean up on your own, I'll leave you to it while I scrounge up something to eat."

And if I couldn't he would what? Strip and join me? Rub soap all over my body with his bare hands to make sure I'm nice and clean? The possibilities are endless and tantalizing.

I poke my swollen eye to remind myself that now is not the time. "I'll manage, thanks."

He strides away before I can argue, shutting the door behind him.

I look in the mirror and wince. "Shitballs."

Shit is what I look like. My hair—usually styled in thick waves that nearly reach my shoulders—is a nest. The light brown is dark with sweat and dirt.

It was an alley. You hope its dirt.

One sleeve of my flannel is torn at the shoulder and a few buttons are missing, but right now I'm more concerned about my face. I've never had a shiner before. Another first. My laugh becomes a moan as I cup my cheek. My jaw hurts and the inside of my cheek is cut, which must be where the blood came from. There's also some bruising around my neck, but that's it. It could have been so much worse.

I turn on the shower, strip and step beneath the spray, hissing when the water hits my side. There's some bruising there too, and I feel like I was kicked by a mule.

Or a jackass.

"I hope your balls fall off, Billy Ray," I growl and reach for the liquid soap on the shower caddy. Luckily, I remembered his name was actually Brent by the time we reached the station. Billy and the Asshole, aka Brent and Eddie, should be getting a visit from the men in blue by morning. So will Toni, if she's still at her apartment.

I wash slowly, unable to stop myself from recalling what she said the last time I saw her.

"Maybe you should call for a ride. My treat."

I laughed as she hovered in the doorway. "What's wrong with him? Can't he drive?"

I stopped rolling up the sleeves of my flannel and let my eyes go abnormally wide. "Is he *old enough* to drive, Toni? Did you set me up with a high school freshman again?"

She shook her head with a small smile at my teasing. "He was eighteen and you know it."

"So you say," I teased. "At least he had a driver's license. I know, because no decent pizza place would hire a delivery boy who didn't."

She rubbed her temple and I noticed the shadows under her eyes. "Are you sick, T? I can stay home. I know you arranged this, but we can always reschedule."

"Stop trying to take care of me," she said, almost angrily before pushing her hair back and taking a calming breath. "You're constantly helping other people,

65

people you don't even know, and you never think about yourself. You need someone special in your life as much as your readers do. Someone to take care of *you* for a change."

"Well, maybe this guy is the one."

"He's not." She shakes her head, a moment of panic flaring in her eyes. "This guy is a few hours and an article at most, and if anything about him bothers you, I want you to promise me you'll come right home."

"Yes, mother."

"Good. But once he's out of the way, you should find someone. A serious someone. I don't want you to be alone."

"Don't worry about me, T." I shrug and flex my biceps playfully. "Even if I'm alone with my hand for another decade, I'll survive. My shelf life is eternal. Like a Twinkie."

She didn't laugh. "I want you to be happy, JD. One of us deserves to be."

I get a face full of water and shampoo as I shake my head. "Damn it, Toni."

She'd been doing so well. She was saving her money and daydreaming about an island vacation, her too-skinny frame was finally filling out to form healthy curves. I thought she was moving on.

I should have seen it.

I've always had a talent for reading people and situations, discovering what's going on beneath the surface. When I was younger I used it to entertain classmates and make teachers uncomfortable. It didn't win me a huge assortment of close friends though. Mainly because I couldn't *stop* doing it. Watching. Observing. Combine that with my lack of filter and you've got a weird, socially dysfunctional child that makes people uncomfortable. Matilda told me I'd either be an investigative reporter or an FBI profiler. She was hoping for the former, since she didn't want me working for "the man".

But maybe I'm slipping. I didn't see the trap they laid for me tonight. I didn't see Toni's setback, and it must have been coming for weeks. Now I'm naked and bruised in the shower of a man whose intentions are unclear or, at the very least, confusing. Why am I having such a hard time reading him?

I can see the basics. White knight syndrome isn't unusual with first responders and the military. And he's lonely. He's left everything he's ever known behind for something new. Which for me is normal, but for a guy like him? I get it. It's a big change.

What I can't wrap my head around is the way he's treating me. The way he was treating me all night, even before I got my ass kicked. The looks, the touches, the overly attentive behavior. It's more than kind. It's protective. Almost possessive.

You're seeing what you want to see, Green.

That's what I'm most afraid of. My reaction to him could be clouding my judgment, making me see a connection that isn't there. Objectively, we don't have much in common. He's bossy. Older. Intense. Probably irritatingly punctual.

Even if he is gay or bi, he might not want anything to do with me sexually. For all I know, he could look at me and see a child. A young recruit that got into a fight because he mouthed off and now has to be reprimanded. To take his punishment from the hot, older drill instructor by stripping and bending over the—

Not going there tonight.

A wave of exhaustion and dizziness swamps me and I turn off the tap. Definitely not going there. I don't think I could if I wanted to.

"Damn," I swear softly and hobble out of the shower, wrapping the towel around my waist before leaning against the cool counter.

"JD?" the words come with a knock and the door opens before I can respond. "I brought you food and something for the pain."

It would be easier to fight this attraction if he'd quit being so *nice*. "Thanks, but anything stronger than aspirin and I'll have to pass. Trust me, you don't want to see me on pain killers."

His eyebrows go up. "They don't knock you out?"

"There are nurses in a certain Seattle hospital that wish they did."

He covers his smile by scratching his beard and I'm struck again by how attractive he is. Too attractive. There is such a thing, and he's a prime example of the breed. I know my limits, and he is too much for me to handle.

I'd still love to give it a try.

"Good thing I brought whiskey," he says easily, stepping closer and eyeing my naked torso with concern.

It makes me self-conscious. "Do I look that bad?"

Dark eyes flash with something that disappears too fast for me to identify. "The bruises look painful. Are you sure you don't want to get them checked out?"

"I'm tougher than I look." Truer words. "At least I

can still move all my fingers and toes. And I feel better now that I'm clean. Great water pressure, by the way."

Great water pressure?

A grunt is the only acknowledgment I get as he bends down beside me to rifle through the cabinets beneath the sink. His head is too close to my—*towel*. And what's under it. I need to think of something else before he gets a show he might not appreciate.

"After tonight I'd say security is the right choice for your second career." I look toward the door so I won't think about him being on his knees. "I was out of it at the time, but I could tell by the sound of the high-pitched screaming that you were impressive."

"I barely touched him." He sounds disgusted. "Man took one look at me and had a fit."

Who could blame him? "Whatever you did, it worked. All *I* had up my sleeve was a good tongue lashing, and that only ticked them off."

"I heard some of it." I can feel the heat of him against my bare legs. "Ballsy. Stupid, when you're cornered like that. But still ballsy."

I shake my head wearily. "Stick with stupid. I don't know where it came from. I was mad at myself."

"At yourself? Why? You didn't attack anyone."

"Exactly." I scowl at the memory. "I tried to fight back, but I had no idea what I was doing."

"It was late. You'd been drinking and you were outnumbered."

"You managed."

He pauses at that. "I've had years of training."

"So you're saying I have to join the military."

"No. I'm saying I can teach you."

Those words send my already simmering arousal into the danger zone. *Down, boy.* "Tempting, but I think it's obvious I'm not fighter material."

"Not that obvious, but you don't need to be a fighter, JD."

"Then what are you planning to teach me?" I smirk. "Or do you just want the chance to call me grasshopper?"

"You caught me." Carter's eyes sparkle as he stands and sets down his supplies. "You could fight, don't get me wrong. But I can show you how to protect yourself. Escape holds, disarm attackers, things like that."

"Still not convinced since I'm also not big on crying." He frowns and I find myself staring at his Adam's apple so I don't have to meet his gaze. No one has an attractive Adam's apple. Was he made in a lab?

"What do you mean?"

"Your friend Brady? You made him cry." I hold up two fingers. "Twice."

When he bites his lip I want to lick it better. "I won't make you cry, Green. I promise."

I think you will.

His gaze captures mine and I can't look away. I've never been this into anyone. It's like I'm teetering on the edge of a cliff, my stomach dropping to the floor while the room spins.

"Easy now." He catches me before I drop and walks me over to the bed. "I shouldn't have kept you on your feet this long. Tanaka won't forgive me if I lose his favorite advice columnist before my first day on the job."

My body leans against his without my permission. He's so warm. "I'm tired, Zeus. That's all."

"Mildly concussed is more like it," he says in a rumbling rasp, sitting us both down on the bed. "Maybe more than mild, if you can't remember my name."

"I remember everything. That's what I thought the first time I saw you. That you looked like Zeus." *Big Daddy Zeus.*

His rough fingers pinch my chin carefully and turn

me toward him. "How old are you?"

"Twenty-six. You?"

"Forty-three. I was joining the Corps the year you were born."

"At seventeen? Is that allowed?"

"When you want something bad enough, there are ways."

I can see that about him. I *like* that about him. "Desert Shield?"

"No brain damage for you." He seems surprised. "How did you know?"

"My uncle died in the Gulf the year after. I heard bio dad was never the same."

"*Bio* dad?"

I wet my dry lips. That's the last thing I want to talk about tonight. Why did I bring it up? "You mentioned food and whiskey?"

He blinks, his long lashes distracting. "Shit, I did. Sorry about that. You really do need to eat something." He reaches for the food on the bedside table. "Take it slow now. Eat first, then you can have the whiskey while I see if anything needs patching up."

Carter holds the plate for me while I grab the most perfectly cut sandwich I've ever seen in real life. I'm not exaggerating. This doesn't look like he slapped something together for an injured stranger. It looks like one of those beautiful but poisonously glued together commercial sandwiches that are meant to make you crave one certain processed meat above the others.

I bet I wouldn't find a single wrinkle on his sheets either. It's a good thing he hasn't seen my bed. No matter what I do it always ends up looking like it's been hit by a tornado.

I need to stop thinking about messing up his sheets.

It isn't until I swallow my first bite—and get over my self-pity about how painful it is to eat with a recently punched jaw—that I focus on my taste buds. "Wow."

"All I had in the fridge was leftovers. I should have thought of that on the way home. I hope it's okay."

"Are you apologizing? *This* is your version of leftovers? It's exactly what I needed to make everything better." I chew on the barbecued pork and swallow with a groan. "No joke, this might be the best sandwich I've ever had while mildly concussed. And the flavors are so... Did a new restaurant open up around here recently?"

"No. Why?"

He doesn't know me yet. Doesn't know about my

secret stash or my recipe collection. "I need more of this sauce. I'd love to get the recipe. I don't think I've ever had better, and I'm a barbecue snob."

His smile is wider than I've seen it all night. "Glad you approve. Unfortunately, Gran asked me to take that information to my grave. But I can make some fresh and bottle it up for you to take home."

Is this real life?

Carter Willis makes barbeque sauce. This glorious, bearded Marine makes my favorite condiment and looks like my favorite wet dream. Oh and he saved me from the asshole brigade and smells like he'd taste delicious.

If I knew for sure he wouldn't freak and I wouldn't pass out, I'd get down on my knees to thank him properly. With my mouth. As it is…

"Did we just become best friends?"

His shoulders shake, and I know he got that movie reference. By the time he hands me a shot-worth of whiskey we're both grinning like idiots.

I think we did. I think we just became best friends.

Dear Diary,

I want a dirty one-night stand with my best friend, Zeus.

CHAPTER FOUR

Sometimes all you want in life is to cuddle up on your couch and binge-watch your favorite shows, taking the occasional break to eat or jerk off to fantasies of last night's rescuer until you feel better about the world.

And sometimes shitheads trash your apartment and you realize that isn't going to happen for a while.

If you cried, this would be the perfect time.

"Why you, Mr. Lumpy?" I whimper, leaning back on my slaughtered, stuffing-oozing couch and petting it pathetically. "Why did it have to be you?"

I catch Carter—aka my new bodyguard—out of the corner of my eye, and I'm not surprised to see he's still steaming mad. Things are bulging and pulsing that don't normally bulge or pulse on the human body. It's intimidating and wildly erotic, but still. "Why are you mad? They didn't stab *your* ugly couch and steal *your* ancient PlayStation."

But of course Carter is mad. My protection is his main priority. At least, it has been since last night. And let me tell you, he's taking his job seriously. So seriously I'm kind of losing my mind over it.

This morning was a good example. I'd woken up in a strange bed to a whole new world. My clothes had been washed and neatly folded so I'd have something to wear after my shower. Then I'd come downstairs to the smell of Italian sausage and scrambled eggs so fluffy they practically floated into my mouth.

I wallowed in the five star service, trying to ignore how guilty I felt for putting Carter to so much trouble. Then he started poking and prodding my injuries, interrogating me about my apartment's security, and all the guilt was gone. When the answers I gave didn't impress him, he'd insisted on driving me home and following me inside to check things out.

I wasn't sure why he was bothering, but I wasn't going to argue about spending more time in his company. Not when he'd looked even better this morning than he had last night.

I didn't expect what we found when I opened the door. Who in the hell would expect something like that? But Carter's reaction didn't give me the opportunity to slip into shock. I was too busy watching him.

He'd stared at the mess for a full minute before turning around and making a few angry sounding phone calls in the hall—leaving the door wide open to keep an eye on me at all times.

Like I'm five.

By the time police arrived, I was vacillating between irritation at his high-handedness and sexual attraction for the pacing, controlling, overprotective beast. Yeah, I know, but I can't help it. Everything about Carter does it for me.

"This happened *after* they attacked him last night and after we filed the report. Are you telling me they aren't in custody yet?"

He wasn't yelling, but he had his, "Drop and give me twenty" face on and the young officer on the scene looked like he might piss his pants. "Not yet, sir. We've managed to get a hold of a cousin, but he hasn't heard from them and thinks they might be staying with an unknown friend. Laying low."

My sigh is loud enough to draw their attention.

"What about Toni?"

"Your neighbor? She's missing too. Her apartment looks like it got hit by the same tornado yours did, but half the clothes in her closet are gone, as well as most of her toiletries. That gives every appearance of someone packing to leave in a hurry."

At least he let her take her clothes. From the stories she'd told me, he wouldn't have wanted to see anything she'd gotten without his explicit approval. Asshole. "Any signs she left against her will?"

Dark eyes snap to me but I keep my attention on the cute cop. "We can't rule it out, but with their history and her hand in last night's attack it doesn't seem likely." He offers me a sympathetic smile. "I know you've said she was a friend, but in long term abuse cases like this, people rarely act in the best interests of their friends and family. It's not a conscious decision. Just survival instinct."

I know that, but I don't want to believe it, especially not about Toni. "I wish I knew if she was alright."

I wish I'd been able to see what was happening before it was too late.

"You're a good man." He moves forward to pat me awkwardly on the shoulder. "I guarantee we'll do everything we can to find all three of them."

I'm about to thank him when his hand disappears and a wall of flexing back muscles encased in another snug t-shirt obstructs my view. Does he buy them a size smaller on purpose or something? Showoff.

"If you're done here, JD needs to pack a few things so we can go."

"Go where?" I'm not sure what he's talking about. I'm too busy being mesmerized by his exceptional...trapezius? Is that what it called? Whatever it is, I like it. I think I need to take an anatomy class or three so I know exactly what I'm drooling over. Maybe he'd donate his body to my research.

"R-right," the poor guy stutters. "It's pretty clear who's responsible, even if we didn't have witnesses in the building who'd seen the men coming and going. We'll update the APB, and I'll need Mr. Green to make a list of anything damaged or missing."

He's already told me the likelihood of getting anything back is negligible. Why do I have to make a list? Salt for the wound? Way to rub it in my face that when the two imbeciles hadn't been allowed to hit me as much as they wanted to, they'd taken their thwarted angst out on my furniture. And my dishes. And my television...

I stand and move around the obstacle that is Carter Willis with my attempt at a grateful smile. "I'll do that first thing. Thank you for the fast response."

His grin is relieved. "Anytime, Mr. Green. By the way, I love your work. I never miss your column, or any of your diaries. It's amazing how you can manage to be so funny and compassionate at the sam—"

Before he can finish, Carter is herding him out the door. "We'll be in touch with the list and for an update on the manhunt."

That was rude.

And hot.

But rude.

"Is it the uniform?" I ask lightly as I pull the irritating hair away from my face with a rubber band, grab a garbage bag and start to pick up pieces of broken plate and glass.

"Is what the uniform?" He leans against the door, rubbing his palms over his face as if he's still tired.

"Do you see a uniform and need to make it cry out of some deeply ingrained training, or is it something else?"

He glares balefully in my direction. "This is a crime scene and he wasn't taking it seriously."

"My couch was murdered, how serious is that in the grand scheme of things? And I think he was taking *you* seriously. Especially after you name-dropped the old chief of police a few dozen times."

"He was about to ask you for an autograph. Or a date."

"He was about to ask for advice, Zeus. Flattering me about my writing was the first clue. My work is funny and compassionate? He never misses a column?" I curl my lip. "Yeah, he's got sex on the brain, but I'd bet good money that he doesn't want it with me."

I'd also bet he wasn't gay. Hetero guys ask for advice all the time. Usually a friend turns them on to my column, and they like it enough or are desperate enough to ask me for help. I don't mind and I love a challenge. As they say, love is love.

"Someone asking for a date wouldn't flatter you?"

I can't stop my snort of disbelief. "Not like that."

"How then?"

I'm *not* reading anything into that question. He's not asking for himself. Nope. But the topic he's broaching is a sore spot for me, so it isn't likely I'll keep my mouth shut either.

"You want to know about the mating habits of

today's gay bachelor? I've spent the last six months researching the subject. As far as I can tell, it consists of Photoshopped dick pics and Grindr hookups. Screw pointless praise not pertaining to the peen. They get right to the point and ask if you want to *cum* over." I emphasize. "If it's yes, you go back to their place. If you're not feeling it, you move on to the next dating app—and there are dozens—or you can play it safe and phone a friend. Fuck buddy," I clarify. "But that's more like a *break glass in case of emergency erection* situation. Never a date."

Carter's face mirrors the disgust I feel.

"I know," I say with a gusty sigh. "And don't get me started on the well-meaning coworkers and matchmaking hobbyists that have set me up since I started the diary, not thinking I need to have *anything* in common with their choices other than my orientation. This is why the Dry Spell Diaries exist in the first place. When you start to look for a genuine connection to go with your booty call? That's when it all goes to hell. The deeper I've gone down this rabbit hole, the more I believe that dating is the root of all evil."

"None of what you described sounds like dating to me, Green. Dick pics? Fuck buddies? I'm not saying I haven't had a few one-night stands in my life, but they shouldn't be the norm. What happened to dinner and conversation? Hanging out and letting nature take its course?"

Sounds good to me, but I'm discovering I'm a dating traditionalist. "Nature apparently takes too long. You have no idea how many men I've met in the last few months who told me that all their previous long-term relationships started as random hookups. Sex was their introduction. Finding out if they could have a conversation with each other came after."

He shakes his head. "I must be older than I thought."

"I wasn't going to bring it up."

"What a sweetheart," he quips.

I start tossing things in the trash, trying not to smile as he throws back my sass from last night. It's helping. I need something to distract me from what used to be my happily cluttered apartment.

They're only things, I tell myself. Cheap things and I didn't have much of them to begin with. Nothing that can't be easily replaced.

I can't lie. I *am* a little upset that my laptop was smashed.

I set it gingerly on the couch and Carter's brow

furrows. "I'll call Tanaka again. He can salvage what's in there and set you up, good as new."

"That's a nice thought, but I think this one is a lost cause." I don't want him to know how close I am to losing my shit. "I already have everything backed up on the Cloud anyway. Online," I say when he frowns in confusion. "All my work is backed up online."

Speaking of work, I'm going to have to tell my editor about Toni. He'll be shocked when he hears what happened. He knew her background and worried about her as much as I did.

Maybe she's already called him. They used to talk on the phone all the time, so at this point he might know more than I do.

Carter joins me in my trash collection, studying the room as if looking for a place to start. "How long have you lived here?"

I glance up and know what he's seeing. One room. One Mr. Lumpy. One narrow bed that doesn't look like it could fit two people, let alone five like his. And before it was kicked over and destroyed, one giant ass flat screen. Because priorities.

"Home sweet shoebox? I've been here ever since I moved to town two years ago. I didn't need much space and the price was right. It helped me pay off my student loans a few months back, so now I'm rolling in...well, I don't like to brag. Let's just say I could buy a new television today if I wanted to. With enough change left over to do my laundry."

Yeah, I'm still a broke-ish twenty-something and college was expensive. There were scholarships, but in order to survive with a full course load so far from the family fridge, I'd needed help. By the time I graduated I had enough debt to choke a miniaturized pony and two degrees that at first glance didn't translate into high paying jobs.

I think I managed okay.

"You've already paid off your loans? I thought you were still in school." Carter lifted the shattered screen back to its stand so he wouldn't step on it. "Fiona mentioned something about a class you took together last semester."

I go to open the cabinet under my kitchen sink, the one where cleaning supplies are usually stored, and I'm grateful to see all my old textbooks still present and accounted for. I wait until he's looking my way and show off my collection.

No, I don't have bookshelves. Did you miss the part

where *I live in a shoebox?*

"We're perennial study buddies," I answer. "Technically I graduated a few years ago, but I can't seem to give it up. It's my one true vice. Other than *Netflix*. It could be worse, right? Some people are addicted to porn."

I notice his eye twitch. "Is that face you're making because I'm a nerd, or are you one of the people addicted to porn? It's okay to tell me. I'm a professional. I get paid not to judge."

"Neither," he says severely. "Yes, to be honest, hoarding that many textbooks under your sink could qualify as nerd territory. And I have watched more than my share of porn because there's not much else to do for entertainment on the base. But that's not what I was thinking about."

Can I ask what kind of porn?

No. No you can't.

"But you *were* thinking about…?" I press instead.

"I've considered going back to college once or twice myself. Not for a degree or anything, but because I wanted to learn something new. I was thinking that's something we have in common."

This intrigues me more than I can properly express.

"Name something you'd want to study if you could."

"Art history, maybe?"

"Really?" That was the last thing I was expecting him to say. How can the man keep getting sexier? It's got to be a statistical improbability.

Carter nods slowly, gauging my reaction. "I've seen some beautiful things in this world. Carvings in the middle of the desert. Cave paintings and museums that are older than our Constitution. I always wanted to know more about them."

I find myself wishing I'd traveled more and seen some of those beautiful things with him. I want to sit him down and make him describe every one in detail. I want to rewind the moment and record that wistful quality in his voice when he tells me about his secret love of art again.

The more I learn about him the more he confounds me. Every time I think I have him pegged, he throws me for a loop. A manly, heroic, art-loving, Kung Fu-quoting, neat-freak, barbecue-infused loop. "I'd take that class with you."

"Yeah?" His grin is contagious.

"Absolutely. It so happens I hoard textbooks and always have an opening in my schedule for a new class."

"Nerd."

We're smiling at each other, but after a second or two I need to look away or I'll start begging for a hug. Or a backrub that could lead to dry humping. *Some* sort of physical contact with this man who pushes buttons in me I didn't even know existed.

I shouldn't go there. I'm having a hard enough time as it is—pun intended—trying to hide my reaction to him. The one that won't go away, no matter how bruised I am or how ransacked my apartment is.

I really need some alone time with my hand to sort out my feelings.

"Damn it." Thinking of masturbation reminds me I'll have to throw my sex toys away. Whether they were touched or not, I'll never be able to use them again without wondering. Thinking about that helps to turn down the volume of my sex drive.

Carter comes over to grip both my shoulders, offering me a supportive squeeze. "They're going to find them, Green. Bet on it."

"I'm good." I try to shake off my mood and not collapse into a defeated heap on his chest. "It could have been worse. Shit happens, right?"

One big palm slides around to cup the back of my

neck and I almost moan at how good it feels. "It shouldn't happen. Not to someone like you. Someone who was only trying to help a friend."

I look away to hide the need his words and gentle touches are creating inside me. "I hear good intentions pave a certain road."

"Stop doing that."

"Doing what?" Leaning into him like a greedy sex fiend?

"Every time you get a compliment, personal or professional, you brush it off. That's a bad habit you need to break."

I'm not as good at taking advice as I am at giving it. I know this about myself, but it doesn't stop me from bristling. "Is this how you made the ginger giant sob? Empathy? Because I was imagining more of a Richard Gere, military montage scenario. A pushups in the rain, face in the mud, nowhere else to go kind of thing."

Carter scowls, hand tightening reflexively on my neck. "You keep bringing that up. It was my job to help young Marines who'd never faced true violence survive the real thing and come out the other side intact. So yeah, I was hard on them. Pushing people to their emotional and physical limits had a purpose, but I wasn't doing it for personal enjoyment, because I'm not a damn sadist. I'd like to think it kept a few of them alive. That was the point. To make sure they came home to their families."

"I'm sorry, Carter," I offer, guilt lowering my voice and tying my stomach in knots. "I'm being a jerk when all you've done is help me."

His expression softens as he lets me go. "You're allowed. You've been through a lot, Green, and you've managed to keep a smile on your face through most of it. And you're still thinking about your friend, worried about her, even though you have every right to be angry. You're handling all of this better than most would in your situation."

I've got him fooled then. I don't feel like I'm handling it. I don't want to handle anything. In fact, I'd really like to hide from everyone involved for at least a year. Including him. *Especially* him. "Thanks to you. I won't forget everything you did to help. And I'm *never* forgetting your grandmother's delicious barbecue sauce. Once things settle down here, I'll meet you back at Finn's and ply you with the best in beer and peanuts until I can convince you to be my personal Mr. Miyagi and secret sauce supplier. Deal?"

It's an obvious opening for him to leave. I'm giving him an out so he can go home and stop worrying about me. He's earned it. There's no reason for him to stick around and watch me try to sew Mr. Lumpy back together along with my pride.

If Matilda taught me anything, it was the importance of standing on my own two feet. Self-reliance. No man has the right to define me. No man needs to protect me. I'm a strong, independent woma—man. Independent *man*.

She had a hard time remembering to adapt her female empowerment speech for her horde of foster sons. Which might explain why we all grew up to be slightly confused, if well-educated supporters of womankind. Luckily Rick was around to… No. The history professor and unapologetic feminist was no help in that department either. Good man, though. Always had a smile on his face.

The opposite of Carter's expression at the moment.

"Why wait? We can talk more about it tonight. Pack enough for a few days," he orders.

I sit down stubbornly and cross my arms and legs, hoping to hide the tent my pants just made in response to his command. "I think I'll stay and get the place back in order instead of heading to a hotel. My landlord is going to have a fit when he sees this mess and finds out about Toni's apartment. I can't afford to lose my deposit if he kicks me out."

"I've already talked to him. He's not kicking you out, but he *is* going to come in here with his maintenance guys tomorrow and fix anything that's broken."

"*You* talked to him?"

There's not an ounce of guilt in his expression. "In the hallway while the officer was taking your statement."

I'm thinking a normal person would be insulted instead of aroused. "A little presumptuous of you, Master Sergeant Willis."

"I'm not denying that. Now do you pack your things, or should I?"

Gorgeous, bossy bastard. "I know where you're going with this."

He crosses his arms as well, biceps bulging and ready for the battle. "Where am I going, Green? Enlighten me."

"You asked for it." I give him my best side eye. "You feel responsible since you saved me, and guilty that you weren't there sooner. The idea of leaving a bruised up kid in a trashed apartment is offensive to your sense of honor and decency. I can appreciate that, but allow me to alleviate your concern. I'm great." I glance quickly around the room and correct my statement. "As soon as I buy a new television, I'll be great. I've never had a problem looking after myself, so the care and feeding of Ken's favorite columnist is covered. I cooked breakfast for a dozen people every morning for years before I graduated high school. After that, ordering takeout should be a snap."

I don't tell him who those people were, or that half the time Pop Tarts and frozen breakfast burritos were on the menu. He doesn't need to know everything. "I'm good," I repeat firmly. "You're absolved. Released. Your karmic spreadsheet is balanced. I. Am. Fine."

"But are you done?"

I chew on my lip, thrown off balance by his quick comeback and enigmatic expression. "For now."

"You're not fine," he calmly corrects me. "And repeating a thing doesn't make it true."

I try to respond, but he holds up his hand, determined to make his point. "You told the police that Toni has a key to your apartment. You've admitted it's possible she's with the men who attacked you, who might have done worse if they hadn't been interrupted."

I really don't want to think about that.

"They aren't in custody yet, which means they could come back at any time and there wouldn't be anyone around to stop them."

"Bet you're a joy at Christmas parties," I mumble bitterly.

Carter shoots me a stern look. "You want a bright side? Let's say they're smart and they stay away. You'd still be here on your own. You said you'd be fine as long as you had a new television. How exactly would you manage that? I know you won't take pain meds, but there's no way you could drive responsibly when you're banged up like this. That is, if you had a car. Do you have a car, JD?"

"No." Am I shrinking? Can he still see me on the couch or do I look like a smallish speck of lint? "I was planning to call for one."

He nods grimly. "Sure, that would work. And would you trust a stranger who pimps out his car to help you back up the stairs while carrying your purchases? Would you let him in your apartment? I'm curious, since I already know you wouldn't ask a friend."

"How do you—"

"You haven't called anyone since last night, Green.

Not at the police station and not this morning. And judging by your stubborn insistence that you can take care of yourself, I doubt you'll send up the bat signal once I've gone." His breath comes out in a gusting sigh. "So *your* plan is to sit on your murdered sofa that's surrounded by broken glass, with nothing to distract you from worrying about your neighbor and what part she may or may not have played in what happened to you. Did I miss anything?"

"You forgot the takeout."

"Shit, I did, didn't I? Nobody's perfect."

"Is this what I do?" I mutter, uncomfortable at being so easy to read. "I don't think I like observant people."

"Well I don't much care for the fact that you were right about what *I* was thinking either. Most of it," he amended. "I do feel guilty for not getting to you sooner. My friends and I are the reason you didn't leave at a decent hour, so one of us should have made sure you were safely on your way home. And *anyone* with an ounce of decency would hesitate before letting you deal with this mess alone. But I don't see you as a kid, and I don't think you're incapable of taking care of yourself. I'm not asking you to come with me out of pity or a sense of obligation."

"Then why?"

I feel more than see him move closer. When I lift my chin his eyes are already on me, clear and honest. "I enjoy your company, Green. And despite you being stubborn as hell about accepting help, I wouldn't mind a little more of it. You already know my place has enough room for you to spread out and spend a night or two. At least until you get your locks changed. It seems like the smartest solution to me."

What he's saying makes sense. He has the room and he wouldn't mind the company. Those are reasons I can understand, even relate to.

When I don't respond right away, he brings out the big guns. "I also thought it might be nice to have Fiona and the guys over for barbecue tonight, since my recipe got rave reviews. I haven't had anyone over for dinner since I moved in, so I'd appreciate the extra set of hands. You'd be doing me a favor."

I squint at him, my injured eye throbbing in time to my rapid pulse. He's wily. I wasn't expecting that. "You're using Finns, Fiona and your grandmother's magical sauce to get me to do what you want? That's manipulative. That's bribery."

"That's friendship. Particularly when your friend is

being too damn contrary to do what's in his best interests."

He sits down beside me and I suck in a shaky breath when his hip grazes my thigh. I can't dismiss my reaction to him when he's this close, and it doesn't have anything to do with friendship. It could be an issue if we spend more time together. Who am I kidding? It's already an issue. "I'll be honest, Zeus. I'm not sure staying with you is what's best for me."

Carter lifts his hand, gently tracing my sore jaw. "These are the facts. I'm not leaving you alone until the idiots who did this are in police custody. Simple as that. It's not happening. So either I'm staying here and sleeping in…" he looks around dubiously. "*On* the floor. Or you're coming back home with me."

His gaze drops to my lips and something flares to life in his eyes, making our situation harder to deny. Since I woke up, I'd been trying to defuse my reaction to him. Telling myself he reminds me of my foster parents. Those two would bend over backwards to save a troubled child, and I think Carter would get along with them. They're practically the same age.

But despite his reasoning and mine this—his touch and the way he's been treating me? It feels like attraction. As in not parental. As in mutual.

As in still delusional?

Maybe. Either way, what in the hell am I supposed to do with that?

I give my trashed apartment another quick glance and shake my head. The facts, he said. The fact is I don't want to stay here alone just to prove I can. He's right. I'm not in any shape to accomplish more than brooding over what's already happened. I've got no computer, no flat screen and no one I'm willing to call and whine about my life to.

Usually, I'd suck it up and deal, but when it comes down to it, I think I'd rather exist in a state of semi-permanent arousal from his heated glances and constant attention than cuddle up for the night with nothing but my wounded pride.

Screw pride, anyway. At least for another day or two, give me a protective Alpha male that smells like sex in the woods and wants to make me dinner.

Sorry, Matilda.

"Only for a night," I finally concede. "Two tops. And we'll be making a few stops before we go back to your house. There are things I need."

"What are we getting?" He doesn't conceal his

surprised smile. I think he was expecting more of an argument. "I already have a television, so you don't have to worry about that right now."

"I'm getting a new laptop and a few gallons worth of Moose Tracks," I tell him. Maybe some lube, if I can sneak it by him. "And I'm buying the groceries for dinner. It's the least I can do and it's nonnegotiable."

I can tell he wants to argue but he wisely decides against it. "As long as I can carry the bags and there's a pint of pistachio, I'm in."

"Our friendship is over. Pistachio?"

"Like Moose Tracks sounds so appetizing?" He counters with a chuckle as he stands there, hands on his hips like my own personal superhero.

I'll convert him. He'll be as obsessed as I am by the time I'm through with him.

Are we still talking about ice cream?

Maybe. All I know is my sex drive is back with a vengeance. In case anyone was worried about that.

CHAPTER FIVE

"I think I accidentally activated my second phone tree in your honor, Green." Wyatt glances up from his plate, barbecue sauce coating a bashful smile. "Though if anyone asks, I'm blaming Seamus for both of them."

"What does that mean, exactly?" And what was his first phone tree about?

"I told my cousin what happened to you. He told his husband, who called Ken. Of course he and Brady had already heard about it from Carter, so as we speak they're installing security cameras and getting Trick— that's one of my cousin Jen's guys—to recommend someone who can keep an eye out as well."

"That's…" Confusing, probably expensive and fills me with guilt. "Wow, okay, I'm not going to ask about your cousin having multiple guys because that would be inappropriate, but the other thing? That's a bit of an over the top response for one freak occurrence. Did you explain the fact that it happened *because* of me? If I'd changed my plans and not gone to the pub for my da—"

"I hope you're not trying to say any of this was your fault," Fiona interrupts severely. "And you can't count him as a date anymore, either."

"No, but maybe it's—"

"Maybe it's my fault." Wyatt is no longer smiling. "I knew there was something off about him. He was too jumpy. I should have knocked that punk on his ass instead of asking him to leave."

"It wouldn't have changed anything, Wyatt. There was no way you could have known what he was planning. I didn't see it either, and I'm usually good at sizing people up."

I keep remembering the nerves Brent exhibited, the way he held his phone so tightly I was surprised it didn't crack. But that's normal for a blind date. None of it screamed, "I'm holding you here for a friend so we can use you as a punching bag."

"Extra measures are a good idea." Carter isn't looking at me when he responds. "That's what I told them when Brady called to let me know why they couldn't make it tonight."

So that's why the couple hadn't shown up. I'm not upset about it. I feel comfortable with these three, and it's been a long time since I socialized on a regular basis. A regular *not for an article* basis.

But I'm wishing the topic of conversation wasn't so depressing.

"I love that bar," I sigh. "I'd hate it if what happened ended up changing the atmosphere." No matter what they say, that would be my fault. *My* bad judgment. *My* mistake.

"It won't change anything at all, JD. Okay, maybe the cameras will put a stop to the unmonitored sex in the alley," Fiona adds with a grin. "But Finn's isn't a quiet little pub anymore. Not after all the renovations Seamus has made. With the label taking off and the place being packed more often than not... More people should mean more security. I hear that's good business."

Wyatt used his napkin to wipe his lips with a bit too much care before turning his attention on Fiona. "Had a lot of sex in the alley, Fi?"

She chuckles and pats him on the arm. "Not me, firecracker, but if *you* haven't then you might be the only

Finn who missed the boat." She catches me smiling and arches her slender brows. "Here's a scoop for you, Green. Wyatt's family is predisposed to a certain behavior we professional headshrinkers like to call exhibitionism."

"Who can blame them?"

"Exactly. They're all so naturally gifted, of course they'd want to show it off." Her smile is wider now. "You would be shocked if you knew how much time I spend warning people not to take their breaks out back when a Finn is in the house. But I have to admit, I enjoy it so much more when they don't listen."

"I'm shocked." I'm not. Not at all. I've heard the kinky whispers. Even Senator Finn's wife was rumored to be a real wild thing before the wedding. I doubt being married with kids has changed her *that* much.

I feel Carter's knee accidentally brush against mine and imagine him cornering me against a wall somewhere public where the two of us might be discovered. The idea of him being so impatient to claim me that he can't wait until we're alone, that he'd want everyone to know exactly who I belong to…

I adjust myself under the table.

I can see the appeal.

"Let's not write about that scoop, okay, man?" Wyatt includes me in the glare he's directing at Fiona. "My family doesn't need any more notoriety. Not about our...not about *that*."

I mime locking my mouth with a key and throw it over my shoulder. "This dinner is off the record."

He nods and swiftly changes the subject. "Carter, you should come to the next Finn Again. I bet Brady would like it. He already thinks of you as family."

"He— Yeah? Maybe I will." No one else notices, but I can see that telling twitch near his eye that says he's flustered. Surprised. Why would he be surprised? He has to know how much Brady admires him.

"If you made this you'd have a standing invite, and I'd have someone to talk to who isn't otherwise occupied." Wyatt pauses and shakes his head. "That was rude, wasn't it? I didn't mean to assume you weren't... If you're seeing someone, you could absolutely bring her to dinner, man."

Carter quirks his lips. "Don't worry, Wyatt. You're right. I'm not in a relationship at the moment."

He's looking at me when he says it, and I'm doing my best not to read into every move he makes. "It must be hard to be one of the few remaining single guys in the family. Too much PDA with your pasta, buddy?"

Wyatt nods but Fiona makes a scoffing sound. "Don't let him fool you. I've been to one or two of those dinners myself. He loves teasing his family about their public displays. It's the babies that bug him more than anything."

"Fiona."

"He doesn't know how to act around toddlers he isn't rescuing from burning buildings, and he still isn't used to his brother being a single dad."

There's a tightening around Wyatt's mouth and tension in his shoulders as soon as she mentions his brother. Why? I don't know enough about them to guess and it makes me wildly curious.

Why can't life be like a television show? Watchers usually get to know what's going on well in advance, even if the characters haven't found out yet. I *hate* not knowing things.

"Zachary's a cute little guy." Carter throws in, unaware of the undercurrents he's paddling into. "I've seen the pictures Brady has on his phone. And Noah's a good man to take that on by himself. Not many men would do that."

Wyatt leans back in his chair, glowering. "He's

always been a good guy, but he had no idea what he was getting into. Seamus makes it look easy, but it's not. One reckless fling at a wedding and he's changed everything about his life basically overnight. Up to and including his shifts at the firehouse, because juggling his schedule with a baby was too much for him to handle alone."

"I hear that's what babies do," Carter says in a quiet, non-confrontational voice I can't help but admire. "Change everything overnight."

"But he's not alone. In a family like yours, you're never really alone," Fiona assures him, her forehead creasing at his tone. "And now he's got someone with experience there to watch Zach and get things organized, so it should get easier."

But it wasn't the same. Wyatt doesn't say anything but his face is easy for me to read. "Big families aren't always a cure-all, and having one doesn't mean you never have to work through certain things on your own," I say absently, staring at Wyatt when he looks up as if surprised I'm taking his side. "Sometimes they cause more problems than they solve."

"Damn straight."

"And the larger the family, the harder it can be, if you don't agree with the majority. But just because something's right for them doesn't mean it's automatically right for you. At least, not on their timetable."

"Right?" Wyatt puts his hands up and looks at me as if I'm a genius. "See, he gets it. If you don't stand up and cheer every time someone upends their life without warning, even if it's a decision you don't understand, you're the bad guy."

"I do get it." I offer him a supportive smile. "And you're not the bad guy, Wyatt. Personally, I think Zach is lucky to have an uncle like you. An uncle who can teach him how to make his own decisions. How to handle himself when the unexpected throws him for a loop. Someone needs to, don't you think?"

Wyatt's expression goes from startled to considering. "Yeah, I guess you could be right. Sneaky, what you did there, but I see your point. I'd do a better job than the rest of my brothers, that's for sure."

"I'm sure you would, and I'm always right. It says so in my bio."

I feel Carter studying me again, but I manage to resist meeting his gaze.

"JD knows a lot about big families." Fiona says suddenly, turning the spotlight in my direction. "What did you tell me again? *Ten* foster brothers?"

"Nine." I wish she hadn't brought it up. Talking about my family gets…complicated. "But only one of them is married with kids so far."

And since Craig's high school sweetheart-turned wife thinks we're a family of misfit toys and I live on the other side of the country, all "Uncle JD" knows about them is that they take adorable Christmas photos.

"*Nine brothers*?" Carter asks in disbelief. "Is that what you meant by that breakfast comment earlier? I had no idea."

All eyes are on me now, and my face heats from the attention. "We haven't had a lot of time to swap family tree info. It's not exactly something you bring up in casual conversation."

"Unless you're Fiona," Wyatt mutters.

"Unless you're Fiona," I agree with a sigh. Apparently I'm not the only one that wasn't born with a filter.

"Fine." She rolls her eyes. "Blame me for wanting to have stimulating dinner conversation about what it was like for the two of you growing up with so many brothers in the same house. Wyatt has five of his own, you know. You could have compared notes. Never mind.

Let's all stare vacantly at our empty plates instead." She instantly looks contrite at her outburst and offers a tentative smile to Carter. "The plates are empty because the food was delicious. JD was right about your *special sauce*."

I cough into my hand.

"It's not really mine, but I appreciate it." Carter hesitates, glancing at me from beneath his lashes before looking back at her. "I was an only child, so I can see the fascination. I used to wish I had a houseful of brothers and sisters."

"Thank you." She gives us a speaking look. "I'm glad someone at this table understands me."

"We understand you." Wyatt snickers and reaches for his drink. "And if you're both that fascinated with big families, we can give you a couple of brothers, right, Green? Hell, I have a trio of cousins fresh off the boat that are turning into real troublemakers. They'd probably take one look at Carter and be willing to call him daddy if the price was right."

"Ice cream." I push back my chair with more force than I intended. "I think it's time for ice cream. Fiona, come help me."

Carter starts to stand. "I can get the dessert."

"You made dinner."

"You bought it."

"You saved my life."

"Hardly," he huffed. "But if we're going in that direction, you should be taking it easy."

He's killing me and I either need to run away or jump him. "I'll survive the trip, Carter. Keep Wyatt company. We've got this covered."

When I finally get to the kitchen and open the freezer, Fiona is already leaning in close to whisper, "What is going on with you two?"

"*I don't know.*"

"I'm serious, tell me."

"*I'm* serious. I've got nothing." I pause, tilting my head as if considering. "I don't think he needs Wyatt's cousins. I've already been adopted."

The sound she makes says she's not buying what I'm selling. "He's not looking at you like a father would, JD."

More like a daddy.

Stop thinking like that, freakazoid. "Have you heard anything about his personal issues or preferences?"

"Not really. He's only been coming around the bar for a couple of weeks, and I've never seen him with anyone but Brady and Ken. I do know his parents are gone and he didn't leave any kids behind. I remember Brady mentioning that as a selling point for getting him to move here. Instant extended family."

Just Lonely gets another point in its favor. "There you go. That's what I thought. He's being a nice guy and getting company in the bargain."

"That is *not* the vibe I'm getting."

Me neither. I think about today at my apartment, and ask before I can stop myself. "What's the vibe?"

"Sex, genius. The vibe is all about delicious, dirty sex."

"And here I thought it was all about dinner."

She shakes her head. "Not unless you're the one on the menu. He's barely noticed we were here all night. He's been too busy defiling you with his eyeballs."

I wrinkle my nose. "He's an eyeball defiler? Way to suck the sexy right out of that sentence, Fiona."

"Speaking of sucking, you stink at reading people when it's about you and your neglected dingdong."

"Classy, but point taken." I take out the ice cream while she finds us bowls. "It's a good thing I'm brilliant at it when other people are involved." I lean closer. "So why are *you* being such a dingdong?"

"What do you mean?"

"You're acting like you don't want to light up that sizzling firecracker currently attached to your hip when we both know that's not true. So what's with the friend zone bullshit?"

Fiona stares at the pistachio. "It's complicated."

"Your *Facebook* status is complicated. But what's the reason? Is it because you work for his family and things could get awkward? Is it because you don't like men in uniform? That can't be it. Who doesn't like a fireman's uniform? There's an entire calendar industry devoted to them."

"Of course I like his uniform," she hissed. "Why the hell are you talking about his uniform? What does that have to do with *anything*?"

I shrug, fighting my grin. "Just trying to dig out the truth. You like him, you love his uniform, and he's got a great family. Oh and he's pretty too. You'll have to help me out, Fiona. I'm not seeing a downside."

"What if the downside is that I'm kinky, free-spirited and slightly poly by nature and he's...pistachio? This *is* pistachio, right?"

"Yes, but Wyatt isn't." I knock my hip with hers. "What he is, my fellow philomath, is eager, trainable and

113

smitten."

She tries to hide her smile by playing with her lip ring. "Did you say smitten? Out loud?"

"It's a valid word."

"For a historical romance. Or Scrabble."

"Don't try to change the subject by mocking my vocabulary skills."

Her smile disappears and her shoulders slump with a sigh. "I don't know, JD. He doesn't adapt well to change. I thought he did at first. The rest of his family is great at going with the flow. But then Noah showed up with the baby and... If you knew more details you'd understand."

"I think I've gotten the gist. All the men he's grown up with are starting new lives with their significant others. Half the guys he used to cruise for ladies with are now more interested in men. Babies are popping up all over the place. And didn't you tell me about a recent death in the family?"

"His father." She nods thoughtfully.

"*His father died*," I emphasize. "It doesn't matter whether their relationship was good or bad, that's not an easy thing to deal with. Believe me, I know."

"And right after that, his oldest brother resigned from

the force and came out to everyone." Her whisper is so soft I have to strain to hear her.

The old chief of police came out? O-kay. That family is fascinating, but whatever, it helps with my narrative. "So in that big family where everything is changing *but* Wyatt, would it be safe to say he might feel like he's getting left behind? I mean, I don't have a master's degree in psychology or anything but—"

"Shut up." She nudges me with her elbow. "You helped him in there, by the way. He wasn't thinking about the fact that he was an uncle. Now he is."

"Of course he wasn't. It sounds to me like change has given him all stick and no carrot." I lean my head on her shoulder playfully to lighten the mood. "He needs you to be his carrot, Fiona."

She pushes me away with a soft laugh. "I'll give you a stick right in the eye if you don't stop."

"It's too soon for eye poking jokes." She looks up at my black eye, so distressed that I wrap an arm around her. "I'm kidding. I'm sure I'll be able to see out of it again eventually. As long as you take my advice." She stares at me blankly until I shrug. "What? You know I'm right about the carrot."

"How about this? You deal with the May/December

thing you've got going on with your Marine, and I'll find a way to deal with Wyatt's carrot in my own time." She steps back, gathers up two bowls and walks back to the table before I can respond.

Please. May/December thing? Carter isn't eighty for God's sake. And there isn't *a thing* to deal with yet. It's just dinner and a sleepover. For the second night in a row. With a guy I had a sex dream about last night. A guy who keeps touching me and feeding me and apparently defiles me with his eyeballs when I'm not looking.

Oh hell, there *is* a thing. There's a big, giant thing and I have no idea how to deal with it.

"It looks like you lost your helper. Mind if I step in?"

The spoons in my hand clatter to the counter. Carter is too damn stealthy for my peace of mind. "I'm good."

"Are you sure?"

I glance at him over my shoulder and hum thoughtfully. "I think so. Unless you want to take a bite of my ice cream and admit it's better than yours and I'm always right about everything."

"Everything? You sound pretty confident I'll like it." He chuckles and moves closer until he's standing right beside me. "I guess you better let me have a taste so I can judge for myself."

I guess you better let me have some privacy so I can rub one out and be near you without limping.

His eyes stare pointedly at the spoon that's back in my hand. He wants me to feed it to him? Is he trying to torture me?

Maybe I'm into that, because instead of handing it over or teasing him about being too old to feed himself, I wordlessly dip it into the container and then up to his lips.

What the hell are you doing, Green?

I'm blaming his mouth for my bad judgment. His salt and pepper beard usually distracts me from it, but this close I can see how generous his lower lip is. For all his sharp, masculine features, the man has ridiculously feminine eyelashes and a mouth that begs to be kissed.

The smile he makes before the spoon disappears in his mouth is genuine and irresistible. And when he swallows and groans out loud? If he does it again I might come in my pants.

"Damn, you might be right, JD. That's delicious."

"Yeah?" I murmur, unable to look away as he licks a trace of it off his now shimmering lips.

"Oh yeah."

I'm gripping the spoon so tightly I'm losing feeling in my fingers. *Don't touch him. Do. Not. Touch. Him.* "Good enough to share your grandmother's secrets with me?"

"I thought I had to admit you were right about everything." I can feel his breath on my temple. My cheek. "Are we changing the rules now? And if we are, is that really what you want instead?"

"What else?"

He's so close now his lips are almost brushing mine. "Maybe if we put our heads together we could think of something we'd both enjoy."

This is what Fiona was talking about. The sex vibe. As in my body is vibrating with the need to have raunchy, gritty sex with Carter Willis.

"I'm not sure we'd, uh, enjoy the same things."

"You might be surprised."

I bite back a gasp when the front of his jeans brush against mine, telling me what I most wanted to know. He's hard. Huge and hard and close enough for me to grab hold of.

He's as turned on as I am. And he's definitely interested.

"You're really going the extra mile to keep that

recipe to yourself," I joke weakly, not sure what to do with this erection information.

"And you're tempting me to give it to you. But I want something in return."

Yes, give it to me. Take whatever you want. I breathe out on a soft moan, my hips tilting forward without my permission until I feel it again. *There.* Jesus, it's a beast. There's a fucking steel Leviathan in his pants and I need to see it. Try to wrap my fingers around it. My mouth.

Carter grips my wrist and lowers it to my side, the spoon dropping unnoticed to the floor. "Are you going to give me what I want, JD?"

He's still close enough to kiss, but he's restraining himself, as if waiting for me to make that final move.

I want to. Jesus, how I want to. But for some reason, like an idiot, I lean back instead. Away from his lush, sensual mouth. Away from temptation. "Shouldn't we get back to your company?"

Coward.

His expression is tight and his fingers flex around my wrist. "If that's what you want."

I *want* him. What the hell is wrong with me? "Carter, I—"

"*Again, Fi?*"

Wyatt's angry words shatter like breaking glass around us, ruining the moment.

"You're ditching me for Thor again?"

"Who's Thor? Any relation to Zeus?" I sound a little manic as I slip away from Carter and move unsteadily toward the couple heading to the door. "And where's the fire? Shit, wait, is there an actual fire?"

I just realized there are some expressions you shouldn't use around firemen.

Fiona's smile is brittle and polite. "A text from a friend. He needs some help studying for a final exam."

"Bullshit." Wyatt's expression is the definition of frustration. I can relate. "He's always studying for a final. Or he needs you at the bar. No one works as hard as Thoreau Wayne at finding excuses to see you."

"Except for you?" She challenges him before hugging me gently, almost apologetically. "Sorry, hon. I'm glad you're in good hands. And how about the next time something happens to you, you feel free to give me a call, okay?"

That's not the first time she's mentioned that tonight. "I will. Drive safe."

"I'm driving her," Wyatt says, his frown grim. "I'm free tonight, and I've got nothing better to do now. I might as well help my cousin's business partner pass his damn final."

"That's probably not a good idea." My radar goes off at her tone. Why is she telling him not to when she knows how he'll react to…?

Oh.

"Two heads are better than one," I offer, trying to help without being obvious.

Two heads. That's what you're after with that reverse psychology isn't it, you kinky poly girl?

"See? Green agrees with me." Wyatt sends me a grateful wink. "It's settled. I'm coming."

Fiona glares in my direction but all I see is, "Thank you."

And you're welcome. One of us needs to get lucky tonight.

Wyatt might get that carrot sooner than I thought.

By the time they thank Carter for dinner and say goodnight, I have enough self-preservation to have moved out of his reach. I'm at the stairs before he turns around to face me. "Dinner was great, but I think it wore me out. I'll make up for the dishes at breakfast, okay?"

I don't wait for him to respond before I disappear.

Don't you mean run away like a headless chicken?

I'm not afraid. I just need a minute because Carter blew my mind. I hadn't seen it coming. Not like that. Not during dinner.

One minute I'm doling out ice cream and unsolicited advice, the next I'm a heartbeat away from humping Carter's leg like a sex-crazed, six-foot Chihuahua. And if I'm not mistaken, and I know I'm not, he was *fully* on board with that plan.

Are you going to give me what I want, JD?

If he'd taken without asking, I wouldn't have stopped him. It never would have crossed my mind. But he did ask. And something made me hesitate. Something I'm already regretting, since none of my doubts matter when they come up against this need he makes me feel. A need he might already be on his way to taking care of if my fears hadn't gotten in the way.

I close the door to the upstairs bedroom and lean heavily against it, unbuttoning my pants with quick, clumsy fingers.

"Carter," I groan and jerk my dick out in rough desperation. Fuck, I can't remember the last time I was this hard. So hard it hurts. I close my eyes and in my mind I'm back in the kitchen. Only this time Carter is kissing me and it's his strong fist I'm fucking my cock into. "Yes."

Fiona and Wyatt laugh softly in the dining room, adding to the thrill I get when he turns me and bends me over the kitchen counter.

"This is what I want." Without warning he drags my pants down to my thighs and spreads the cheeks of my ass with his strong hands. One thick finger traces the crevice between my cheeks and makes me gasp. "There it is. This ass. I've been thinking about doing this all night."

"You have?" I groan into the countertop as that now magically lubed finger pushes against the tight ring of muscles until I can feel it inside me. Opening me. Filling me. "Oh God."

"Oh yeah. Look at that. So tight and hungry, the way it's already sucking me in. You're going to give it to me, aren't you, JD?"

"Please, yes. Take it. Do it."

"Do what?" But I can hear the smile in his voice. He knows exactly what I want because now there are two fingers filling me. He's getting me ready to take his big cock. Ready to be filled and fucked. God, I'm so ready.

"Tell me what you want me to do, JD. I need to hear you say it."

"Fuck me. I need you inside me."

"Not yet."

My frustrated moan has him laughing. "You'll get my cock when I'm ready to give it to you. You can wait. You'll enjoy it more if you wait."

"No I won't." I don't want to wait. I can't. Not when there are people in the other room that could walk in any second. Not when he's fingering me deep enough to lift my feet halfway off the floor. "I'm too close, Carter. You have to...you have to..."

"Have to what? Do whatever I want to your body? I agree. I saved this ass. It's mine."

He removes his fingers and I feel a new kind of sting as he spanks me once. Twice. "Say it, JD."

"Yours," I gasp, half-crazed now. "It's yours."

The head of his erection gliding against my ass is my reward, sending rippling shudders through my body. "Please."

"What can I do to you?"

"Anything you want."

We both let out a deep, needy groan when he pushes inside me, reaching around to stroke me again. His hips set a hard, unforgiving rhythm that sends me closer. Closer. "Carter."

"Anything I want." His voice is deep and commanding in my ear. "I could keep you tied to my bed, ass in the air, prepped and ready to take my cock whenever I get the urge. And this feels so good I'd want it all the time. I'd fuck you so deep and so often you wouldn't be able to get away, even if you wanted to."

"Oh God."

"You don't want to like that idea, but you do. I can feel it. You need to be claimed. You want Big Daddy Zeus to fuck you hard all day, and then tuck you in and keep you safe at night. Is that it, Green? Am I right, baby?"

"Yes!"

"That's good," he groans, his thrusts more erratic. "So good, taking every inch for me."

I can be good. I can take all of it. More.

His fingers are so tight they're bruising my cock now, his hips jarring me with each powerful stroke. "Give it to me, JD. Come for me now. Only me."

I bite back my cries of release and come hard all over my hand. Wave after wave of white hot, piercing pleasure leaves me strung out and clinging to the door, reeling from my climax.

Holy shit, that was intense.

My head tips back while I catch my breath. Fantasy Carter was a little darker and a lot more possessive than I'm used to. He wanted to own me. Keep me. Tie me to his bed.

Tuck you in. Keep you safe.

I'm not ready to delve into my subconscious about it, and in real life, I might take issue with that kind of manhandling, but I can't deny it made me come like a fucking geyser.

I go to the bathroom, strip and clean up the mess I made of myself before slipping into bed to stare at the ceiling.

There are no roadmaps for this. Or if there are, I don't have them. I'm thoroughly lost when it comes to dealing with what Carter brings out in me. The lust that makes me forget my name. The connection, despite our differences, that I can't remember having with anyone else.

And I can admit now, alone in the darkness, that I'm scared of it. Terrified of seeing where it goes *and* of never knowing. Of things happening too fast or not happening at all.

What's really messing with my head is how right and normal it feels to be here with him. Having dinner.

Letting him take care of me.

It shouldn't be normal. It should be alien and strange and uncomfortable. I'm not a spoiled, helpless child. No one needs to take care of me. I should be dying to get out of his hair and away from his perfectly cut sandwiches and his constant attention. To get back to my regularly scheduled programming.

But I'm not. I like his hair. I like everything about him. I enjoy being with him nearly as much as I want him.

I feel safe with him. I like that too.

That's too much "like" for only a day and a half—but then again, in that same time I've been ditched, punched and burgled. Maybe that's all this is. Emotions run high in situations like this. It makes sense that I wouldn't be acting like myself. This is all textbook, I'm sure. It will pass.

Even as I'm reasoning my way through the crazy, I know that if he puts the choice in my hands again, I won't be able to walk away.

Are you going to give me what I want, JD?

My dick stirs to life again and I groan, slipping my hand beneath the sheets as Fantasy Carter makes another appearance.

127

I'm getting the feeling this is going to be a long night. And that The Dry Spell Diaries might be over soon.

My editor will kill me, but at least there's a chance I'll die happy.

CHAPTER SIX

Writer's block. The struggle is real and it sucks hairy balls.

I came downstairs to write after hours of tossing and turning. Correction. Hours of dirty, twisted jerkoff sessions followed by more sexually arousing angst about a certain bearded drill instructor. Same as the night before.

At the rate I'm going I'll be heading to the ER after all, only it won't be for my fading bruises. *"Mr. Green? Can you tell us how you sprained your wrist?"*

Wouldn't that be a fun story to share with my readers? Nope. Never gonna happen. Sex *will not* send me to the ER.

Last night I'd run away from my intense physical

ɔn to Carter, and my body has been making me
suṃᴜᵣ for it ever since. Either that or my host is slipping
Viagra into every meal. I haven't had this many
erections in...I can't remember, but I think never
wouldn't be a huge exaggeration. Not even back when I
first discovered the wonderful world of the hard-on.

Finding out your penis has superpowers you can't
entirely control is an awesome, scary and exciting time
in every boy's life. And, at least in my case, I spent an
abnormal amount of time studying those powers.
Finding the right incentive to draw them out of hiding.
Trying to master them whenever I had a minute without
one of my brothers around.

What I'm saying is I should have gone blind. So that
myth is busted.

I'd successfully managed to avoid talking to Carter
about our kitchen run-in, or much of anything else, for
the entire day. He didn't bring it up either. I keep telling
myself I'm grateful. And I am. Really.

Instead, he ordered me to relax and recover while he
cooked, worked out for a few hours in the gym upstairs
and then took some calls in his office. Not that I was
keeping tabs on him or anything.

If I was, I'd know he'd passed on checking out the

new security measures at the bar in order to keep an eye on me—I heard part of that phone call with Tanaka—but I didn't bring it up.

I just wanted to stay in my avoidance bubble, with my perfect host who was a perfect gentleman where everything was perfect.

Denial is a seductive bastard.

I don't think Carter wants to stay in the bubble. Despite his silence, I could sense him watching me throughout the day as well. Wondering. Waiting.

For my part, I did my best to distract myself. I talked to the locksmith and my landlord. I tried to get information from Fiona about her study date with Wyatt and Thor. She didn't go into details, but she didn't sound happy either, which was unfortunate. Not a carrot in sight there. So after that gossip well ran dry, I decided to check in again with my editor.

Toni had finally called him.

"All I know is that she's using her sick leave, JD. And that she'll call back as soon as she can."

"She didn't quit?" That didn't make any sense. Eddie the Asshole would have made her quit, wouldn't he? He inferred as much, and he was willing to beat the shit out of me and toss my place for interfering with their relationship. Why would he let her work around me now?

"No. And she said she doesn't deserve any favors, but she still needed me not to fire her until we talked again." Lawrence sighed. "I told her I couldn't make that promise. Not after what the police said. What her boyfriend did to you. Are you sure you're all right? All you have to do is say the word, JD, I—"

"Wait. That's the only word I'm saying. Wait until we know all the facts." It was an automatic response, but it still felt like the right one.

The facts seem pretty apparent on the surface. She set me up on that date. She disappeared after it happened. She even apologized for it via text.

But she didn't quit her job. The clothes she'd picked out for herself had been missing from her closet. She'd called Lawrence and told him she'd talk to him soon.

And I was a fool still hoping to prove my trust wasn't misplaced.

I don't want to think about any of it anymore. It's too late now to make more phone calls or seek out a noisy distraction. Too late to let myself go round in circles about Toni or Carter, so instead I'm gorging myself on ice cream floats and working on my diary.

Trying to work on my diary.

At least I've already finished this week's advice column. Lawrence said I could skip it while I recovered, but I've never had a problem giving my opinion to the lovelorn and hormone-driven. I could swim in other people's Kool-Aid all day long, banged up or not.

I guess you could say I'm like that one grandmother in the neighborhood who pries out all your secrets with homemade brownies and innocent smiles before telling you who you are, why your decisions are wrong and how to live your life. So yeah, like that nosy grandmother... Only with less mileage and more penis.

Dear Green,

My boyfriend of three years didn't follow me out of the closet and the stress is getting to me. I love him and I want the world to know we're together now, but he says his family isn't ready. It's been four months and I'm worried he's the one with the problem. That he doesn't feel the same way I do. Should I give him an ultimatum or will that pressure him and push him away? How do I keep him and stay true to myself? Signed, Loving Loud

Dear Loving Loud,

I really hope you don't take this the wrong way, because we're all proud of you for taking that step, but you need to turn that volume down for a minute so we can talk.

Coming out is a personal journey and I'm sure you already know it's different for everyone. Yes, be proud you took that step. And yes, your frustration is natural, and he needs to know what you're going through. But relationships only work if that goes both ways. So don't give him an ultimatum without allowing him the time he needs to make his choice on his own.

When you remember that it took you three years, even with a man you loved in your life, for you to finally come out to the world? Four months doesn't seem that long a delay.

Ask me the same time next year and my answer might be different.

Today you need to ask yourself *a few questions. Do you really love him? Does he make you happy? Is what you've built together worth the effort and the patience he's asking for? If yes is the answer, then your next step is clear. If not, then you both have some thinking to do.*

Dear Green,

The straight guy I've been crushing on for years wants to "experiment" with me. I'd like to make sure he enjoys himself so this won't be a one-time thing. What's the best starter plug for a sweet virgin backside? And do you have any special tricks or tips to keep him coming back? Signed, Foreplay For Him

Dear Foreplay,

You've just described the start of the best gay porn ever!

"I'll be in my bunk."

Before we talk about my talent for inserting an old but classic Firefly reference into a butt plug question or the specific toys to drive your straight guy wild, can we make sure the man he's experimenting on is okay if that's all this is?

I'm talking about you. I've been down this road before, and if you aren't careful, you could misread those road signs.

Everyone wants to be the reason someone makes big changes in their lives. We all want to believe that one look, one kiss, one perfect butt plug delivered by us can transform our frog into a handsome and in this case, enthusiastically gay prince.

Life, alas, can be a prick with a twisted sense of humor, and sometimes it'll turn that frog into a morning after toad. You know, the one who acts like you're a stranger or a bug on the bottom of his shoe the next time you run into each other. If you know all this and you're still on board, the best starter plug would depend on how adventurous he is.

Take note: Heterosexuals have personal space boundaries and insecurities about their assholes that we'll never understand. I'm sure that's part of their allure, but it's something to be aware of. Sometimes the most they can handle is a thumb after half a bottle of lube before they have to tap out. Then again, if you're lucky, they're anal savants and the world is your cucumber. Or your vibrating eleven-inch dildo. I've heard it both ways.

I'll leave links just in case.

My advice is fairly straightforward. Some emails I get are deeper than others. Some are raunchier. It's not quantum physics, and I don't think I'm doing anything a good friend with a six-pack of beer and a willing shoulder couldn't in my place, but I still feel like I'm making a contribution to peace on earth in my own small, if occasionally perverted, way. Little ripples, right?

It's the diary that's killing me. I wanted to finish what I started last night for the mid-week edition, but I can't bring myself to do it. Why? Because while I was avoiding my bad date and trying to make my readers laugh at our expense, *he* was quietly plotting the ass kicking he and his friend had in store for me later.

I can't turn that into a witty anecdote, and I don't think the powers that be would enjoy the comic diary of a sex-deprived advice columnist morphing into an afterschool special on bullying. Lawrence would have said so if that were the case. He's not shy about his opinions.

Life is already full of sad stories like this. Where we struggle to overcome discrimination, but it gets better. Where we're more likely to be attacked outside of bars—especially if we're labeled transgender or belong to another minority—but it will get better. Even when the current political climate foments the type of hate that leads to life-threatening consequences for everyone we care about? Eventually *it has to get better*. If we stop believing that, then what's the fucking point?

God help me, I'm starting to sound like my foster mother.

I'm supposed to help with the better bit. At least, that's how I've always looked at what I do. I'm the walking, talking, silver lining product of what happens when things move in the right direction, and I try not to take that for granted.

I don't need to hide my sexuality to gain acceptance or further my career. I don't have to define it either. I'm not a bear, I'm not a twink, I'm not a queen, I'm just JD. Fitting into a particular slot in order to make other people comfortable is no longer required.

Being JD means I watch an unhealthy amount of television, obsess over college courses, paying my bills and the amount of sex I'm having—or not having—with other men. It means I work for an online publication where nearly every writer and editor connected to it is also a member of the LGBT community. It means I'm one of many. Average. And that's the ultimate goal, right?

Despite the recent hiccups and backslides, the world has and will continue to change. *For the better,* because that's the only direction we'll allow it to go. I believe in that strongly. Passionately.

But right now I'm discovering that I might not be the social justice warrior Matilda tried to raise. Because I don't want to talk about my bruises or the fact that them calling me fag while attacking me broke off a piece of my hard candy shell. And I don't want to mention that reaching out to help a friend who'd been abused had backfired in such a shitastic way that it made me lose some faith in my gut instincts.

I just want to find something else to write about. So I'm working my way around my mental block. Brainstorming as I drink/eat/inhale my third float of the night.

I'd have guilt for days if I talked about my close encounters of the Finn kind after they'd taken my experience so seriously. So I can't mention Brady and Ken's chemistry, Wyatt's crush or Fiona's intel about the family's public sex fetish.

I can't even bring up my rescuer without sharing what he rescued me from, which would defeat the whole purpose of avoiding my sorry tale.

Or can I? I start typing without considering what I'm going to say.

I don't want to tell you how bad my date was. I know

I always give you every juicy, embarrassing detail, but you'll have to trust me when I say you don't want to know. I wish I didn't know. In this case, ignorance is truly bliss.

What you do *want to know is that right in the middle of (insert worse scenario imaginable), I was struck by lightning. For the sake of anonymity let's call that lightning Zeus.*

Now I have never been the kind of guy to buy into the Some Enchanted Evening scenario. Don't know what I mean? Watch a damn musical. It won't kill you or make you any gayer than you already are.

BTW, the musical we're discussing today is South Pacific. Rent it or I'll wash you right out of my hair and there'll be no more happy talk. (Again, references you'll get after you watch the movie)

Anyway, when I saw Zeus "across a crowded room" I did what any smart, sane, quasi-capable man would do in that same situation. I made like a Popsicle.

I froze.

There he stood, all my secret fantasies come to life and down from Olympus—even a few fantasies I didn't know I had—and all I could do was stare at him like a hungry kid with his face pressed against the window of a closed candy store.

I had what some would call "a moment." They happen all the time. Sometimes they're moments you wish you could miss and they break your heart, but sometimes they're like that. Like a damn musical. Like magic with a dash of Greek mythology and gay porn. When you find yourself in one of those moments, you have a choice to make. Do you run away from it? Do you wait for it to come to you? Or do you take a chance?

I wish I could tell you I made the right decision. The brave decision. But lying in this diary to make myself look better would defeat the purpose.

I choked. My body was ready but my head was too busy running variables. What were the odds that he was taken? Straight? A something-religious that hates homosexuality? What were the odds that when he saw me he would be struck by that same lightning? That he wouldn't reject me?

I was so busy worrying about bullshit that, before I knew it, the moment was gone. I didn't know if I'd ever see him again, talk to him again, or finally break this never-ending dry spell with anyone else after seeing him. I went to the bar for another round and as far as I knew, he popped back up to Olympus, never aware I existed at all.

The point of my shortest and least amusing diary entry on record is this. Don't be like me. Don't waste any more moments, because you don't know what tomorrow will bring. You could walk away from a handsome possibility at a bar and get mugged in a parking lot. You just never know.

Introduce yourself and be willing to be rejected or embarrassed. Don't worry about the mistakes you've made in the past so much that you make another in the present.

No more watching from the sidelines. "Or all through your life you may dream all alone."

South Pacific again. Couldn't resist.

Damn it, that's got enough cheese in it to clog an artery, but it might be the best I can do skating a sugar high at three in the morning. I slip off my glasses to rub my temples, worrying about Carter's reaction to reading this. Worrying about anyone's reaction to reading this.

No one can ever read this.

I'm about to delete it when the phone beside me starts loudly singing about leaving on a jet plane. I slip my glasses back on and answer before it can wake Carter up. "Royal? Do you know what time it is?"

"Are we taking a quiz? I'm game. In what country?"

"That's never not funny."

"I agree. And I always know what time it is. But you work from home," my brother continues unapologetically. "So it's not like you can't sleep in."

"Is there a reason you're calling so late I'll *need* to sleep in?"

"There is. I got back in town an hour ago and checked my messages. There was one from your editor."

Shit. I forgot I had Royal listed as my emergency contact. He's a pilot living in New York City, so he got drafted due to proximity. "I'm sorry about that. Lawrence is a little reactionary. He had no reason to call you."

"He said you had the shit beat out of you, JD. That sounds like a fairly serious reason."

I sigh and carry my laptop over to Carter's comfortable couch, settling in. "Please don't spread that around. To *anyone*, Royal. You know I'll never hear the end of it."

"Are you okay? What happened?"

"It wasn't as bad as he made it sound."

"It couldn't be or you'd be breathing through a tube.

Why'd a skinny guy like you get into a fight anyway?"

I'd always be skinny to Royal. My brother is basically the Samoan Hulk, and I have a feeling he's the reason no one messed with me in high school. Except him. He messed with me all the time.

"Believe it or not, it was about a girl."

He bursts out laughing. "No shit? Talk about things I wasn't expecting you to say. Anything *else* you want to tell me?"

"No, I think that's it. Still gay. Still fine."

"If you say so." I hear his acceptance, along with the sounds of a coffeemaker turning on. Coffee at this hour means he was overseas.

"Where were you this time, Marco Polo?"

"Iceland. It was beautiful. I took pictures. I also took a week of vacation days before flying back."

"A whole week? Who was she?"

"I respect women too much to kiss and tell." He laughs softly into the phone. "But they, buddy. The right question is who were *they*?"

Why am I not surprised?

"You give new meaning to the term friendly skies."

"I'm living the dream," his chuckle morphs into a yawn. "Hey, bro, I'm beat. Are you absolutely sure you're good out there all by yourself? I have no problem coming down there to crack some skulls. I can call Dickie and Manwich and the three of us can fly out and scare the piss out of whoever decided to mess with you."

Richard and Manuel? The last thing I want is to set those three loose in the city. The damage alone…"Hell no. Do *not* call them. I swear I'm good."

"Spoilsport. Okay, fine, but we should pick a holiday soon and stick to it, yeah? When's the last time the Dirty Dozen were under one roof?"

"Five years," I answer quietly. "It's been five years since we were all together at the same time."

"We need to fix that."

"Get some sleep, Royal."

"Take care of yourself, JD."

I hang up and stare at the phone, lost in thought until a deep voice startles me into dropping it.

"Royal? Is he one of your brothers?"

"Carter." I look up in surprise, suddenly anxious. "Yes, he is. I'm sorry, was I too loud?"

He shakes his head slowly, and then my gaze drops from his face and I forget what we were talking about. What call? What brother? I'm too busy staring at the masterpiece standing in front of me to care.

I don't know how to handle the view I'm getting right now, but I'm glad my new laptop is positioned where it should be. *On my lap* to hide my latest erection.

He's basically naked, wearing grey shorts and nothing else. His hair is mussed. His thick thighs, strong arms and hairy chest are visible, and I see a tribal tattoo on his left shoulder, but I can't tell whether the design is Celtic or Norse. I don't think it matters. All I know is it is working for me. The longer I look, the more it works, and the more I'm worried I'll punch a hole right through the keyboard with my dick.

Carter Willis is a full course meal and I'm a starving man. I want to tug on his thick pelt of black and silver chest hair, lick his sculpted muscles and hang on to those mile-wide shoulders as he fucks me right into the wall.

I'm being inundated with images of all the fantasies he's starred in during the last twenty-four hours. But none of them hold a candle to the reality in front of me.

I pulled away for reasons that made sense at the time. It's too soon, I'm too vulnerable and his intentions are still too murky. But I'm having a sudden, violent allergy to things that make sense, and I did promise myself I wouldn't turn him away again. *If* he made a move.

Make a move, Zeus.

"You wear glasses?" he asks in a deep voice tinged with affection.

I adjust them self-consciously. "Words get a little blurry without them."

"They look good on you." He grins. "Though the purple leopard print is unexpected."

Shitballs. I drag them off my face and fold them, flustered. "My spare. I always pick out crazy designs I'd never be seen in public with. It's my incentive not to lose my more expensive black frames."

"Were they broken from…?"

"I don't think so. But I couldn't find them when I was packing. Hopefully they're just misplaced and they'll show once I get my place cleaned."

He nods and then glances down at my laptop. "Are you still in pain? Is that why you're awake?"

"Not at all." Not in the way he means. My shiner is already fading to sickly yellow with purple accents, and my jaw doesn't ache nearly as much. My lack of sleep is entirely dick related. I lick my lips and try to form a few more complete sentences without the aid of blood flow to my brain. "I was trying to get some writing done but that went nowhere. I'd given up when Royal called to check in on me."

"You told him what happened?" He sits down and I'm surrounded by the scent of woods and warm man.

Help.

"My editor spilled the beans, the drama queen." I shake my head. "We need to have a talk about boundaries tomorrow."

The worry lines on his forehead deepen. "Why don't you want your family to know what happened to you?"

"Most of them are on the West Coast, Carter. Why bother them when there's nothing they can do about it?" He doesn't look convinced. "We aren't like Brady and Wyatt's clan. We don't spend all our free time together or have dinner every week."

Family dinners at our house had always been sporadic, and not only because none of us could cook. Between football practices, piano recitals, science fairs, legal briefs and paper grading... It's really a miracle we ever saw each other at all.

"I heard you say it's been five years since you were all together?"

"We all have busy schedules, and a handful of us are out of state, so we each go home when we can, which is rarely at the same time. But if I needed them they'd show up fast enough. Heck, if I told Rick and Matilda, they'd end up coming just to lead a protest outside the police station. Get the local news involved. Which is another reason I haven't called."

"Rick and... Your foster parents?"

Hell.

"Yes. They raised us."

"All ten of you." He still looks stunned by the number. "How did they end up with so many kids?"

It's been a while since I explained my family to anyone, but for some reason, it feels natural to tell Carter. "That's my fault. I was their first. They were best friends with my mom and dad in high school and, after they died, Matilda and Rick took me in and gave me a home."

"How old were you?"

"Four by the time I moved in. When I was six I noticed we didn't have any extended family, so the three of us took a vote and decided to make one of our own. Matilda never does anything small, which is how I ended up with nine brothers. A new one every year, all around my age." I smirk because I know how insane it sounds. "We had another vote when I was fourteen to stop her after Christopher showed up. An even dozen in one house was enough."

"Ten *teenagers* at the same time, no less. They must be saints." He laid his arm over the couch behind me, his words careful. "All fostered? Were they not able to legally adopt any of you? I'm sorry, I'm just not sure how all that works."

"No, it's fine." The question makes that old wound ache again. "In every way that matters, they're family. You hear about those nightmare foster home stories, but we genuinely lucked out. And Rick inherited a giant house with some land, so we weren't suffering at all. But adoption wasn't an option, no."

"So then, JD Green…"

"The name I was born with."

I can do this. I can sit in my pajamas with a half-naked man and chat about my strange family like we're an ordinary couple. *Of friends.* Like we're an ordinary couple of friends.

His arm brushes my shoulders and I actually shiver. "Can I ask you something personal?"

"Isn't that what you've been doing?"

"What does JD stand for?"

"My name? That's your personal question?"

"It is if you don't want to tell me."

"You'll laugh."

"I won't."

Everyone does. But it's late and my defenses are down and he smells amazing. "I'll give you a Jeopardy hint. I'm named after a rebel without a cause."

He laughed. "James Dean? You were named after the actor?"

"That's right. The porn star came around much later. But you lose points for not answering in the form of a question. Who is..." I fade off with a wink.

He leans back, scratching his beard thoughtfully while my fingers curl with envy. "I'm assuming there's a story behind that."

˙ "I guess there would have to be."

His hand drops to my back and he starts to stroke it in soft, gentle circles that I feel everywhere. "Tell me a story, Green."

How could anyone say no to that voice? "Once upon a time, or somewhere in Washington circa nineteen-ninety, my mother finally went all the way with her boyfriend after graduation. It happened at the old drive-in that was about to be torn down. *Giant* was playing. It's an old movie with Rock Hudson, Elizabeth Taylor and—"

"James Dean," he finishes for me. "I know it. Classic

film."

I'm too busy trying not to notice how close he is to be impressed. My skin keeps tingling everywhere he touches me. "Matilda says I was conceived that night and my mother wanted to memorialize the magical backseat encounter, so there you go. The end of a not-that-epic story. I guess I should be grateful I wasn't named after his character, or you'd be calling me Jett Rink."

"Why not Rock?" Carter is smiling again.

"She had a thing for grunge scene bad boys, I hear. The more misunderstood and moody the better. So I got stuck being James Dean Green, or Jimmy Dean Green. Rick calls me Jimmy. But that was worse. I was literally teased about my *sausage* for a full year in third grade before I decided on shortening to JD."

He lifts his hand and pushes my hair out of my eyes, his touch lingering. "James is a good name. It suits you."

"No, it doesn't." How can I think when he's touching me? "James is a rebel. Or a police detective like Wyatt's brother."

"Not a beautiful man who notices everything, with a talent for making people smile?"

Beautiful man. My heart is pounding in my ears at the

compliment, but I try to play it off. "Quid pro quo, pal. There were a lot of famous Carter's around when you were born. Linda, Jimmy, Clarence. Any connection?"

His chuckle sounds like sin. "Sorry. Carter was my grandmother's maiden name. No exciting stories about my conception either. I'm a boring old man."

I could argue that point all night. "Look, Carter, about earlier—"

"Today? When you kept finding ways to avoid looking me in the eye?"

"Yes. No. Not today, but I'm sorry about that. I mean last night."

His gaze narrows in on my lips. "When we were in the kitchen?"

"Right." *Focus, Green.* "That's right, last night in the kitchen wh—"

"When I told you I wanted more?" he interrupts again, the desire in his eyes now unmistakable. "When I almost got a taste?"

His fingers sift through my hair and a whimper escapes before I can stop it. "Oh. Yeah. Exactly... Um, I want to make sure we don't have our wires crossed here. I know you're a good guy and, I mean, you gave me a place to stay and everything. And you seem like an affectionate guy, so touching might come naturally to you. But based on what happened last night and, um, what you're doing now, I *think* you might be letting me know th—oh, God."

His mouth is on my neck; his lips grazing the line of fading bruises around my collar.

Zeus made his move.

CHAPTER SEVEN

"Carter, that feels..." *Yes. Don't stop kissing me.*

"For the sake of uncrossing those wires, I'm telling you that I want you, grasshopper."

My eyes close as tiny shivers of delight streak up my spine. "You had to call me grasshopper."

"You like that?" His laughter is a hot puff of air against my skin. "I wanted you at the bar as soon as I saw you. I convinced Ken to have Fiona introduce us. And let me tell you, I resented the hell out of having to share you with them once they found out who you were. All I could think about was getting you alone, having all your attention, and they refused to take a hint."

"Yeah? Well, I'm glad we cleared that up," I pant, realizing I've been clinging to my laptop when he tugs it away from me and sets in on the coffee table. Then his palm is slipping under my shirt to heat my stomach.

"Is this okay? Me touching you?"

"I don't know if you've read my diary," I joke weakly, head tilting so he can reach more of my neck. "But it's been a while since anyone other than my hand has touched me anywhere."

"How do you touch yourself, JD?" My body almost defies gravity when I feel long, calloused fingers dive down the front of my pajamas to grasp my hard cock. "Like this?"

"Christ." Has anyone *ever* touched me like that? "I, um, I thought I was a pro, but I'm not as good at it as you are. You don't play around, do you?"

"I don't hold back when I want something. Too much for you?" As he speaks, he's stroking my dick like it's his. Like he owns it. It's just like my fantasy. *Better.* "Too fast?"

"No. God, neither. It's… " I turn towards him for a kiss and a slight twinge along my ribcage makes me flinch. Carter notices.

"I know you're better but we still need to be careful." He moves me easily, laying me back on the couch and slipping his fingers into my waistband. "Can I?"

I lift my hips in response and he skims my pants off in one smooth motion. He's good at that.

"Damn, JD."

The way he's looking at me makes my entire body blush. "What?"

His palm caresses my chest, my clenching stomach. "You," he mutters, his whiskey rumble vibrating through me. "You know how much I love art, and here you are. And I get to touch you. Explore you."

I thought the same thing about him, but a choking laugh still escapes before I can stop it. "Are you saying I'm pale and hairless like a statue? If you mention Michelangelo's David I'll get a complex about the size of my pen—"

His silencing kiss is gentle at first. Soft lips brushing, clinging, rubbing against mine. *Sparks.* He sucks on my lips. Biting lightly before soothing the sting. My tongue touches his and he moans and melts against me, pressing me further into the couch. He tilts his head to deepen the connection and my cock jerks against his stomach. Craving more of him. More of this.

This. Fucking. Kiss.

"There's *nothing* wrong with you," he says against my lips when we finally come up for air. "You're beautiful and you feel so right against me I'm having a hard time going slow. Everything about you is exactly what I want. Better than I imagined. Exactly right. Got it?"

My brain is so muddled from that lip lock I'm not sure what we're talking about. *Exactly right.* "Got it. Goldilocks Zone."

"Jesus, how can you be this irresistible?" He's smiling at me, so I must be doing something right. And then his attention is back on my body and his hands are drifting across my skin. *Lower.* "I don't want to push you when you're not ready."

Is he insane? "Do I look like I'm not ready?"

His lips twitch. "Not for everything. Not yet. But maybe you can help me with a problem I've been having."

"Help you?"

"I haven't been able to sleep. I can't stop wondering how you'd feel in my mouth."

"Holy shit."

"I'm assuming that's a yes." His fingers dig into my thighs, opening and lifting them higher. He moves down my body until he's between them. Until I feel his hot breath over my cock. "Yes?"

"Oh my *fucking...*" Both my hands reach for him, fingers threading through his short hair. I need something solid to hold on to. "Yes. It's a yes. *Oh God, Zeus.*"

His tongue is already tracing my shaft, laving the head and humming as he laps up a drop of precum. "You taste as good as you look," he growls. "Knew you would. I want more of that."

"I guarantee you'll get more if you keep doing— *angh.*" I choke back a cry of surprise when he interrupts by opening his mouth over my erection. All of it. He's taking everything. Sucking and licking and swallowing me into his hot mouth and down his throat like he knows what he's doing. Moaning like he's savoring every inch.

I buck against his face helplessly, the coarse hair of his beard scraping against my cock and thighs. His powerful hands are on me, moving me, spreading my legs wider so he can take more, and I'll give it to him. Anything he wants as long as he doesn't stop.

I'm usually the giver when it comes to blowjobs. I'm good at it. Great even. But if I could think at all with his throat closing around my erection and the vibration of his growling moans traveling up my spine I'd be taking notes. So many notes.

Carter is a fucking master.

I'm worried I'll finish too soon. It's been too long since anyone's touched me and he's... "Slow down," I beg. "God, wait, I need to…"

One of his hands leaves my thigh to tug my tight sac away from my skin, making me hiss and groan. He knows exactly what I need. I'm not in charge of this ride at all. He is.

This won't be over until he wants it to be.

"Please. *Please*."

I'm not sure what I'm begging for, but I can't stop the needy noises I'm making with every stroke of his tongue. I want all of it. I want to come. "*Carter*."

He lifts his mouth and his breaths land in rough bursts against my sensitive shaft. "I need inside you."

I tug desperately on his hair when he leaves my weeping cock to go lower, one hand still gripping my balls. Why is he stopping? He can't just stop when I'm this close.

I look down at him with unfocused eyes, sweat dripping from my temples. I don't know whether I'm desperate to come or desperate not to. But if he stops now I might die.

His tongue licks along the seam of my ass and I

almost cry. I'm too relieved to be shocked. He's not gone, not stopping until he reaches—"*Yes*."

I *am* going to die. Combust. Shoot off into space. He's licking and nibbling on my ass like it's his new favorite treat. I feel the scrape of teeth, the rasp of his beard and the firm, wet pressure of his tongue as he pushes inside. A satisfied sound rumbles in his chest, and I know that's what he meant. What he wanted.

I need inside you.

I bite my lip until I taste blood. *No one* has ever done this to me. Spread my cheeks and fucked me with their tongue. Feasted on me like I was their last meal. I've read about it. Talked about it. Watched it. But I've never experienced it before. It feels obscene. Hot, wet and primal. And already better than any sex I've ever had.

His constant growls of pleasure are sending small shockwaves up my spine, intensifying the sensations. My ass rocks against his mouth, begging for more of his thrusting tongue.

Lick me. Fuck me. Please.

He's claiming me here on his couch with my legs in the air and his face buried in my ass. His tongue digs deeper and I cry out.

Again. Deeper. Don't stop.

The electric shocks zapping my nerve endings tell me I'm close, but I can't quite get there. Every time I reach for my cock, he slaps my hand away in warning.

I have to wait. He told me to wait. Zeus gets what he wants, and *then* he'll let me come.

I need to come.

A thick finger joins his tongue and I let out a ragged cry, my head shaking frantically on the couch cushion. "Carter, I can't. That's…" Too much. Insane. Amazing. Full. "More. Give me more."

He groans in approval and adds a second digit, lifting his head to watch them disappear inside me. "That's the sexiest thing. This is what I've been thinking about. Getting inside you. Watching you come apart for me."

"S'only fair," I slur drunkenly, trying to ride his hand. Needing him deeper. "I wanted you inside me as soon as I saw you."

"Is that right?" His fingers thrust deeper. Faster. *Oh God.* "Did you picture me taking you in front of everyone?"

"Yes."

"So did I, at first. But now I'm thinking we'll leave the exhibitionism to the others. I'm not interested in sharing this view with anyone else. This is too good for them. This is just for me."

God, that's hot. "Yes. Yours."

"I want all of it, JD. All of you. We'll have to wait until you're a hundred percent but—"

"What? Why?" Whatever percentage he needs me to be, I'm there. Whatever he wants, I want to give it to him now. Almost as much as I want to come.

A sexy grunting swear escapes him as his fingers thrust and twist inside me. "You aren't ready for what I'd really like to do to this tight little ass. Hell, you might be too young for the thoughts I'm having."

Too young? "Tell me what you want, old man." I'm desperate now. Hotter than I've ever been. "I can take anything you want to dish out."

I can take you.

He drops down to lick me again, adding moisture to ease his way and making me tremble. I groan, my heels digging into his wide back. "*Please.*"

"I love hearing you beg," he mutters darkly against my taint before lapping at my balls with his tongue. He tugs on them again and I shout shamelessly. "I shouldn't admit that. You already think I like to make men cry."

Make me cry.

"I'll beg for you," I gasp out the promise. "I want you

to make me."

He bites the inside of my thigh hard enough to sting. "Don't tempt me. Are you sure you want to know?"

"Yes!"

He licks my skin and moans. "Fuck, you're sweet. I wanted to drop you to that kitchen floor and hold you down. I thought about sending the others away and making you scream my name for the rest of the night, but you went to sleep before I got the chance."

"I wasn't asleep." My nails score his shoulders and arms as I fight to keep myself from reaching for my erection. "I was too busy jerking off, imagining you holding me down."

Carter groans and I bite back a feral smile. "What else?"

He's breathing faster now. Eyes bright with lust. "I wanted to spank you. Punish you for smiling at that cop in your apartment. For coming up with all those reasons to send me away." He sucks the skin of my thigh into his mouth again, and I know I'm a lick away from losing it. "I don't know what's wrong with me. You make me crazy, JD. You're still healing and I want to mark you. Does that scare you?"

Yes. I'm scared of how much I want it. I let him go

164

and struggle to remove my shirt. "Do it."

"Do what?"

It's hard to concentrate with his fingers curving deep, rubbing against my prostate again and again and making me shudder. I'm holding on by a fraying thread and I don't know if I can last, whether he tells me to or not.

"Come on me. Mark me, Carter."

"Jesus," he swears, his cheeks flushed. "You want me to come on your chest?"

"*Please.*"

"Fuck, yes."

With that low, fierce response, his mouth slides down my cock again, swallowing me whole and sucking until I'm writhing beneath him, senseless. Climbing higher and higher as I force myself to wait.

It's only when he lifts his head long enough to say, "Come now, baby," before taking me back in his mouth with a greedy groan, that I finally explode.

Sweet relief. Every cell in my body is having its own mind-blowing orgasm at the same time. Like the full body climax had been building up inside me for all these years, waiting for him to set it free.

Waiting for him.

I watch through a blissful haze as he swallows every

drop of my release, his eyes dark and unblinking on mine, his full lips spread wide.

The image is branded in my mind now. I'll never forget how he looks in this moment. How it feels to be this satisfied. Never.

With one last, greedy lick, he gets to his feet and steps out of his shorts, coming back on the couch to straddle my waist with his thick, muscular thighs.

"Holy Zeus," I breathe out raggedly as I finally get a good look at the beast.

His cock is a world fucking wonder. Every vein and ridge, the flushed color of it, the dark nest of hair at the base and the pearly drops coating its silky head—it's all perfection.

I lick my lips, wondering how he'd taste, and he groans. "Stop tempting me with that mouth. The way I'm feeling now, I'll be too rough on you."

But I want rough.

He starts to stroke himself, looking down at me like a Viking or some ancient fertility god claiming his due. My spent dick twitches instantly back to life. "Do it," I dare him. "No one has ever marked me before."

"Fuck."

My eyes go wide as I see his erection get bigger.

Harder. He likes being the first.

"I'm dying to fill you up," he growls. "To see what you look like when I'm balls deep inside you."

"With that monster?" I eye his length and girth, trembling with arousal. "I love a challenge."

"Not yet." He starts to jerk himself hard and fast, his fist so tight his knuckles whiten while he keeps his gaze focused on me. It makes me feel powerful, the way he looks at me.

My hands caress his thighs. "Not yet," I agree, watching him with unblinking eyes. "But I want you inside me, Zeus. I want that sexy beast forcing me open. Want you to make me take every inch and then call me a good boy."

I can't believe I'm saying this, admitting it out loud, but at my words, everything in his body goes still and tight for less than a heartbeat. And then he erupts.

"JD," he groans. He pumps himself into his hand and jet after jet of his release blasts hot across my chest and chin.

He's stunning like this. His expression is frozen in painful ecstasy, eyes clenched shut and his large body shuddering and flexing with the force of his climax.

I could watch him forever.

I swipe my fingers across the wetness on my chest, bringing them up to suck them in my mouth. God, that's good. Salty and delicious. One taste and I'm already addicted.

He opens his eyes and looks down at me, lips curving softly.

"What? What are you thinking?"

"I'm thinking I need to kiss you again," he says, sliding down and pressing his chest to my sticky flesh. "And it needs to happen right now."

"Good idea."

"You're the one with all the great ideas, grasshopper."

Carter's surprisingly still-hard cock glides against mine and we groan into each other's mouths. He rolls more fully on top of me and his hips start a slow, sensual circle, creating the best kind of friction. The kind that already has me trembling and ready. He smiles against my lips and reaches between us, giving us both what we want. Again.

Well, hell.

He's ruined me. I'm only twenty-six and I'm finished. Done.

Carter Willis is the best I'll ever have.

***

Dear Diary,

I woke up in his orgy bed and didn't want to leave.

I think the only reason I found the willpower to do it was *because* I didn't want to. Some people might think that's backasswards, but it's more about preservation and pride. My pride. My preservation.

And backasswards is a word. Look it up.

I get that I'm making this more complicated than it needs to be, but I've never spent the night with anyone before. Not common knowledge, that's not something I like to admit to, but there it is.

There was this one time I had sex with my boyfriend of the moment on a train, and technically we slept in our seats afterwards, and those seats were adjacent...but it's not the same thing.

So I'm currently experiencing another personal first, and learning I don't handle those as well as I'd like. That doesn't mean I don't know exactly what it is that sent me running this time.

The morning after.

If the sex had been bad, or even slightly satisfying, what happened next would be easier to figure out. But what do you do when you have the most unexpected, unbelievably incredible sex with a man who was giving you a place to crash while you had your locks changed? Someone you've known for less than a week?

How *should* I have responded to waking up sprawled on top of him like a human blanket, with his hand possessively cupping my ass?

There's an obvious answer, I know, and if everything didn't feel so up in the air and rife with potential complications, I might have gone for round four. And yes, I said four. Carter made me come three times before I passed out beneath him on the couch.

Best night of my life.

I'm such a fraud. It's almost laughable to think I've been giving out sex advice for years when I've never actually had it before. Not the right kind. Not *that* kind.

The train guy, one prom night/truck stop/tequila mistake—don't ask. A fellow introvert I met for coffee and wound up dating for two months, mostly via Skype. And Closet Cowboy Rod. Other than the occasional hand job with a goodnight kiss topper, that is the sad sum total of my sexual resume. None of those experiences are in the same *universe* as what Carter did to me.

That was more than good sex. So much more there are no words—and I always have words. But now I'm all emotion and sensation. Altered somehow, and completely at a loss as to what happens next.

So I left the bed, and I'm showering in the guest bathroom while I get myself together, because I refuse to let one night turn me into that clingy guy that won't take a hint and go away. Everybody hates that guy.

Carter hadn't made any noises about wanting me gone. Yet. And the man is relentless and vocal in his pleasure, so I know he's not shy and that he enjoyed last night as much as I did. But that doesn't mean he wants a repeat first thing this morning, if ever. It doesn't mean the two of us are suddenly an item. He's too experienced to be spun by this the way I've been.

I am so fucking spun.

I'm also crashing at his place. Eating his cooking. I know he invited me, but we're still not in an equal-footing situation. If everybody hates the guy that clings, I can only imagine how they'd feel about the one who takes advantage of a generous man.

I stick my face in the hot water and drag my hands through my by now thoroughly washed hair. I can do this. Get myself under control and be cool about last night and all the orgasms. I'll get dressed and call my landlord to make sure he has the new key to my apartment, and then I'll go back to my life.

If Carter isn't up by then, I'll leave him a note. A friendly note with no pressure or strings attached.

Thanks for everything. Last night was just what I needed?

Or *Love your sauce and that monster cock. Hope to get another taste soon?*

Maybe a note is a bad idea.

If he wants to see me again, great. If he doesn't, I'll deal with it. Simple. This doesn't have to be a big deal. I can be an adult about it.

A chill hits my back when the shower door slides open. I turn and nearly fall on my face before two strong arms wrap around my waist. "Carter?"

"You were gone when I woke up." He sounds grumpy, which turns me on if my hardening dick and racing pulse are any indication.

"I—" That's all I get out before he's lowering his head for a kiss.

Yes. Damn, he's too good at this. My cool disappears and my bones and most of my willpower melt away as his scent surrounds me. He eats at my mouth, his tongue teasing and tangling with mine. The delicious scrape of his beard makes me moan as our cocks gravitate towards each other like slippery magnets beneath the pounding spray.

I barely make out the sound of a lid flipping open and there's the thick, cool sensation of lube trickling between my cheeks. His fingers follow, massaging and spreading me before one thick digit presses for immediate entry into my—"*Fuck*, Carter."

He lifts his mouth, his breath ragged against my cheek. "That's my plan, grasshopper. What's yours?"

I shake my head in confusion, unable to focus with his finger curving deep inside me to hit that magic spot. *There.*

"This works," I answer roughly. "I like this plan."

"That's good." He holds me tight against him with an arm around my waist as he plays with my ass. "Between the way you raced out of my room and the bag on your bed, it looked like you were planning to leave without saying goodbye."

"I can't—*Oh*—I can't stay here forever. I'm better now and my locks are probably changed alre—ah, that's good. Don't stop," I beg when he adds a second finger. I try to push back, to take more before I'm ready, but Carter isn't giving me any room to maneuver. He's controlling me. Controlling everything.

That shouldn't get me as hot as it does.

I look up and his eyes lock on to mine. Something in them makes it impossible to look away. "Not yet, JD. Don't run away yet. Be with me today."

The request is raw and sincere, and it tears something open inside me. He wants me to stay, and I need to give him what he wants. That's the only way I can describe it. *I need to*.

He must see my answer, because he lowers his head to my neck and growls out my name. His fingers spear me, stretching me almost to the point of pain, and I still want more.

"Your ass is too damn tempting," he mutters. "I can't stay away from it. All night long I had to stop myself from slipping inside while you were sleeping. My fingers. My tongue. Had to keep reminding myself to wait. You were unconscious and it would be wrong to take advantage of you."

"Are you trying to shock me or make me come?"

"You asked me to tell you what I want to do to you, JD. Last night, remember? Well this morning that's what I wanted. I couldn't stop rubbing this sweet little hole and dreaming of fucking it. I wanted inside. Wanted you to wake up coming for me."

His fingers massage my prostate and my eyes nearly roll back up in my head. "Damn, Zeus. I didn't know a drill instructor could talk like that."

"But you like it." It's not a question, but I'm nodding anyway.

I tremble, my cock throbbing with every scrape of his teeth and lick of his tongue against my skin, every pulse of his fingers inside me. His heart is racing along with mine, and everywhere I touch his muscles flex and roll.

I grip him tighter, crying out when he adds a third finger, the stretch almost too much. Too good. "What the hell are you doing to me, Carter?" I murmur hoarsely. "Other than driving me crazy."

"You think *you're* crazy? I haven't been this hard since I was a fucking teenager." His gravelly chuckle sounds pained. "And what I'm doing is getting you ready for me, as much and as often as I can. When I finally take you I'm not sure I'll have the control to go slow. All I can think about right now is bending you in half, burying myself inside you and just fucking *taking* everything you'll give me. It's not a gentle feeling, JD, but I don't want to hurt you."

I moan at that and he lifts his head, his fingers pumping faster, deeper inside me to touch that perfect spot. "You like that idea, don't you? The thought of me losing control with you?"

His other hand lowers to stroke my cock. "*Yes.*"

"You going to come for me now, JD? Bruise my fingers with it and let me see your face while you give me what I need?"

"*Yes.*" I'm already so close. His words pushed me to the edge. Dirty, delicious words that lick along my skin and set me on fire. But it's something he does with his fingers that finally sends lightning arcing through my body, making me scream. "*Oh God, Carter. Yes!*"

My hips are grinding against his, dick rocking into his fist as I come.

He's still murmuring filthy things and holding me close, but when his fingers slip out from between my cheeks I instantly drop to my knees. Weak after that orgasm. Hungry for him.

"JD, what are you doing? You're still hurting, baby."

I look up at him, the water splashing off his washboard stomach and onto my chest. "You're hurting more. Let me." I grip the silky steel of his erection in both hands and open my mouth over the wide head of his cock, making him groan and stumble back a step to lean against the wall.

"Fuck." His hands cup my head and I can feel the fine tremor in them. I know he's fighting the urge to take over. To fuck my mouth the way he wants to. But he's trying to be careful.

There's some discomfort, but it's more from his size than my bruises. He's so damn thick, my Zeus. I lick and suck and take as much as I can, savoring the salt and heat, the smell of him. He hits the back of my throat and my eyes water, but I won't let go. My hands grip the base of his shaft, fingers tugging on the hair there while I try to make him as wild as he made me.

From the way he's swearing I think it's working.

His fingers flex around my scalp. "That mouth, JD. That fucking mouth," he snarls. "The second you opened it I knew you'd be trouble."

Adrenaline races through me and I'm shivering with it as I kneel at his feet. Didn't I say I'd worship at his shrine the night I saw him? I want to worship his cock. The too-long, too-thick beast that promises pain and pleasure and every damn thing in between.

His woodsy scent is more intense here, mixed with the musk of his arousal. I want to bury my face in it. I want him in my lungs, in my mouth, inside me.

I want him to come.

He presses forward and I choke, breathing out and relaxing my throat as much as I can. "That's right," he rasps. "You wanted me, so take me. Take everything like a good boy."

Christ, he said it. I drop a hand to my newly swelling shaft, stroking it in time with his, too aroused to resist. *Good boy.* Should those two words have that much power over me? Should I be this desperate to hear them again?

"I'm coming, JD. Coming, bab—*Ah.*" He's grunting and groaning so loud it echoes off the walls, his hips rocking in shallow pumps against my face. "So fucking... *Good.*"

Warm liquid heaven spills down my throat and I suck harder, greedy for every drop. I shout against his shaft when I follow him with my own climax seconds later, too turned on to hold anything back.

"You're so damn beautiful," he whispers as he looks down at me and caresses my hair. "And that mouth should be illegal."

When I'm done he tugs me up and into his embrace, half carrying me out of the water before drying us both off. All the while he's touching me, stroking my skin and praising me softly.

Good boy.

By the time he lays me down in his bed—the huge orgy bed I'd snuck out of less than an hour before—my eyes are starting to close.

"You better be here when I wake up this time," he tells me, but I can hear his smile. "If you're not, I'll come after you again."

His fingers caress my ass, cupping one cheek again as I slip into a sated sex coma.

Be with me today.

I'm not going anywhere.

CHAPTER EIGHT

"So you agree?"

Carter nods in resignation, but there's laughter in his eyes. "I suppose you want me to say it."

"It couldn't hurt."

"Fine. Chewbacca carried Han's storyline and Princess Leia was the true hero of *Star Wars*."

I shift against the arm of the couch, slipping my feet back into his lap. "I'm glad we got that over with. Matilda would never forgive me if I didn't make sure Leia got her due."

"I'm still not sure I believe you watch those movies every year just to argue with your mother."

"Well, you don't know Matilda. She argues for a living and loves getting into the details. Since I have no interest in law, I found something we'd both enjoy discussing that isn't my love life or the fact that I live on the wrong coast."

He starts massaging my feet and I adjust the blanket, melting deeper into the cushions with a happy sigh. As far as days go, this one might be the best I've ever had.

I'm saying that a lot, I get that. It doesn't make it any less true. I've had so many firsts and bests in the last few days. Most of them—the good ones anyway—are because of Carter.

After the shower incident, we didn't go back to sleep for long, though we still spent most of the morning in bed. We touched each other and talked quietly for hours, as if we were sharing secrets that someone might overhear.

One secret he told me was that he almost got engaged when he was around my age. She'd been a good friend and all his buddies were getting married or having children. But when he picked up the ring and imagined his future, he realized he wanted something different. Someone different. So instead of proposing, they spent the entire night talking. He told her he was pretty sure he was gay, and that it wouldn't be fair to her, or anyone else, to try and pretend otherwise. She told him she was proud of him.

They still talk once a year and send each other Christmas cards. I can't even be jealous of the woman retroactively. I'm too grateful she'd been there for him.

But for each bit of information I struggle to collect on him, he manages to get reams more from me. I'm starting to get the suspicion that Carter likes hearing me ramble, because every time I try to rein it in or focus on him instead, he asks me another question about a favorite movie or childhood memory.

He even brought me my phone and picked things for me to read from my own advice column. Most of the questions were about sex, of course. He assured me he was taking notes for later.

The one thing he isn't remotely curious about? The Dry Spell Diaries. He shut down both times I brought it up. And I get it. Naked in bed with a guy is not the right time to talk about dates with other men. No matter how bad they were.

We were starving by the time we finally left the bed to put on shorts and t-shirts and make lunch, moving our private party to the couch. But he didn't turn on the television and ignore me. Not Carter. He still wants to talk.

And while he's been keeping me chatting for the last few hours, I've been finding every excuse I can to touch him. I'm feeling the need for another Zeus fix right now.

I tug my foot away from his hand and crawl toward him, all my attention on his perfect, upturned lips.

"I just fed you," he rumbles. "Are you hungry again?"

"Always."

I climb on top of him and his arms wrap around me, arousing and already familiar. I shouldn't get used to it. But damn, do I want to.

His mouth is a drug that makes me lose all track of time. It drowns my senses until all I can think is, *"More."* When I hear his husky moan and feel the erection that's lying like a hot iron against my hip, I slip my hand between our bodies, desperate to touch him. But he stops me before I reach my goal, pulling back to caress my swollen lips with his fingers.

"Either we need to take a break or I need to take up shaving. I'm giving you beard burn."

He manages to sound concerned and proud at the same time.

I prop my arms on his chest, still breathless. "I vote no on shaving. I have a recently acquired beard fetish I want to explore."

He smiles at that, but he looks distracted. As the silence lingers, it dawns on me that he pulled away right when things were getting good. Again. We've been naked or close to it for hours, but he hasn't moved beyond second base since the shower.

If he was feeling as insatiable as I was, I should have beard burn everywhere by now. Is he not interested anymore? Did I misread his earlier request? Or is he trying to tell me he needs a break, but he asked me to spend the day with him so he doesn't know how to say it without sounding like an ass?

I try to move off him but his arms tighten around me. Trapping me. "A break might be a good idea," I say firmly. "Fiona sent me a text a half an hour ago, seeing if I wanted to grab some coffee at the bookstore. I think she wants to talk."

That's not a lie. What I don't tell him is that she didn't ask so much as order, complete with all caps and exclamation points. I hadn't answered yet because I'm being selfish. I didn't want to leave this cocoon of sexual bliss long enough to find out what she wanted. But it might be the smart thing to do.

He scowls when I manage to mancuver myself out of

his arms and sit up, adjusting my stubborn erection with a wince. "You probably have things you need to do that I'm keeping you from. We've been lazy enough for one day."

"No, JD. I don't. I thought we agreed to spend the day together."

His words ease the bulk of my insecurity. Not enough to change my mind, but it helps. "A few hours of break time for my delicate cheeks and your sanity won't hurt either one of us. I could come back and spend the night here if you want m—"

"I want," he says quickly, some of the tension leaving his body. "I want you to spend the night with me."

"Done." I reach for my phone on the coffee table to hide my expression of relief and send Fiona a quick message along with an apology for my slow response.

So I'm spending the night. My third night in a row, but if I'm going to be sensible about this, it should probably be the last. At least, for a while. I'm getting way too comfortable, and the last thing any man wants is an unexpected roommate, no matter how great the chemistry is.

"Eventually, I do need to go back to my apartment. If only to find my good glasses and feed my invisible dog."

I'm going for lighthearted, but my mood takes an unwarranted nosedive as soon as I talk about leaving him.

It isn't a healthy response. People need space. Even in the lusty honeymoon phase of a new relationship, there comes a moment when you need a little breathing room. I'm sure I would advise some "me time" to any *Go For Green* reader in my situation.

But today has been so perfect. It's hard to imagine ever getting tired of spending time with him. Yet another first, because I'm fairly certain I could get tired of anyone.

I look down when my phone pings. "She's on her way. I better get dressed."

This will be good. Socializing is healthy. Everybody needs it.

What you need is therapy, Green.

As soon as I stand up Carter is behind me, wrapping his arms around my waist and burying his face in my hair. "Since you're coming back after coffee, I suppose I could make a supply run to the store for a few ingredients. I'm cooking something special for dinner, and before you ask, it won't be barbecue. But you'll still like it."

I glance up over my shoulder with a grin. "You're pretty domesticated for a career Marine. Shouldn't you have a pantry full of MREs or something? Cans of Spam? How do you know so much about cooking?"

Carter caresses my stomach casually as he responds. "That would be the seventeen years of training I had from two of the finest recipe-collectors in North Carolina. Mom and Gran."

"They taught you how to cook?"

"They taught me everything." He releases me but grabs my hand, walking me toward the bedroom. "Cooking and sewing, hunting and fishing. You name it. And they were always looking for new lesson plans. I once came home to find my grandmother trying to kick a soccer ball around while my mother read her the rules of the game from a library book."

"Now we know why you handled my textbook addiction so well."

His smile is warm with humor happy memories. "That and they were both collectors themselves. Teachers at the local high school. I think they felt bad there were no men around for me to learn from. With their husbands gone, they wanted to make sure I had a well-balanced education."

I stop at the closet where he had me put my bag this morning, implying the guest room was too far away from his bed. "Your father wasn't around?"

"He died when I was three. But before that he'd spent most of my life out of state working on oilrigs, so I barely remember him."

"Me too. I mean, I was three when mine died. Three and a half." He's watching me and I could kick myself for interrupting. "Weird, right? Ignore me. Keep talking."

He hesitates until I motion for him to continue. "After his accident, my mother and I moved in with Gran. They were both devoted to me. I'm ashamed to say I didn't appreciate it as much as I should have when I was younger. But that first leave? My first dinner back home? I realized how fortunate I was to grow up with them always on my side."

"It's hard to imagine a man like you being raised by two plucky widows. You're so…" I fade off and try to encapsulate what I mean with hand gestures.

He smirks. "At a loss for words, Green, or are we playing charades? I'm so what?"

"You know what," I grumble. "I had a foster dad and nine brothers and didn't turn out half as testosterone-y as you did."

That earns me a deep laugh. "I like how you turned out. If your brothers are anything like you, I'm sure we'll all get along."

I glance at him out of the corner of my eye. "Luckily, they never visit me, so you won't have to find out that I'm the weird one. But none of us are anything alike."

"No?"

I find a clean t-shirt and a pair of faded jeans, stripping in front of him. "We're all over the place career-wise too."

"Yeah? Interesting."

He sounds distracted, but this time it's me who's doing the distracting. When I see his unblinking gaze fixed on my ass, I decide not to step into my jeans right away. They'd be a tight fit at the moment anyway.

What was I saying? Right. Brothers. "The only thing we all have in common is our love of strange trivia and the truth. Which is what happens when a civil rights champion and a nutty professor raise a small army."

I shift and sway my ass slightly, my back to him as I pretend to worry a loose thread on the denim in my hands when Carter grips my wrist and spins me around to face him. I love the carnality of his expression. I'd love to see that look every day, and know it's because of me.

Slow it down, Green.

"Any reason you're posing naked when we both know Fiona is on her way to come and get you?"

His gaze drops below my waist, and I reach for his hand and press it against my erection with a groan. God, I love his big, hot hands. "Just making sure you really want me to come back tonight."

He holds me in a firm grip that makes me shiver. "I asked you to stay, JD. More than once. I don't know how to make it any plainer."

Somehow I find the will to back away from his touch. "Good."

Before I can step into my jeans he picks me up and drops me on the bed, his body covering mine. His hips press against me deliberately, pinning me to the mattress. "What is it you're overthinking now, grasshopper?"

"I can't think at all when you're touching me." I wrap my legs around his waist to keep him right where he is.

He grinds against me, his cloth-covered dick dragging against mine. "I don't want you to. Not if it's got you making plans to leave every time I turn around."

"I'm just trying to be reasonable." I'm also trying to concentrate on the conversation, but my hands can't stop touching him. Roaming over the velvet skin of his back, or slipping to curve around the meaty globes of his ass. His body is too distracting.

"Fuck reasonable."

Fuck me.

"I have a lease. And in a few days you'll start working on the job you moved to town in order to take. Whether we want it to or not, real life is going to knock on the door any day now."

In response, he pushes his shorts down to his thighs, so roughly I hear a ripping sound, and grips both our erections in his hand. We groan together. "This doesn't feel real to you?"

His kiss consumes me as our cocks slide against each other inside his tight fist. We moan into each other's mouths at the slick friction, and my fingers dig into the muscles of his broad back. "God, Zeus."

He lifts his head enough to trap my gaze, his eyes so dark with need they make me shiver. "Tonight, JD. Tell me it's not too soon. That I can take you like I need to."

I tighten my legs around him, my body curving so I can look down and watch what he's doing to me. To us.

"You can take what you need now," I gasp. "Anything. I'm good. I'm ready. Nothing hurts. Fuck, that feels *so good*."

"Not now. We don't have enough time for what I'm planning to do to you."

"Fuck plans," I tease, running my fingers through his chest hair and gasping when his grip tightens.

"No time for the meal, but I need an appetizer." He shifts and lifts his free hand to my mouth, pushing between my lips with his finger. "Get it wet."

I lick him, sucking greedily when I realize what's coming, until he pulls it out and places it between the cheeks of my ass. "I need this. Just this and then I'll let you go."

I cry out when he pushes inside, his fist still stroking my cock against his, his mouth at my temple.

"So tight and hot," he growls. "Once I get inside this ass I'll never want to leave. Never want to stop."

I suck on his neck, biting into his skin just hard enough to leave a mark. "Faster. Don't stop."

I close my eyes and lose myself in it. His hand, the feel of his silky shaft rubbing against mine with every stroke. His finger pulses into my clenching hole and I moan his name.

Fuck your good boy, Zeus. Fuck me harder. Don't stop. "I'm close."

"Yes," he whispers, need making us both shake. "I need to feel it, feel you come for me. Then I'll wait. I'll be patient until I get you back in this bed with my cock buried inside you."

He finds my prostate and rubs against it. "You feel that? Right there, JD. That's where I'm spending the night. All night. As much as you can take."

"Oh God. *Carter.*" My body arches against his. Pulsing light and waves of heat shatter me until I'm broken on the bed. I barely hear his shout of release as he joins me, but I feel it on my skin. Marking me the way I'm marking him.

"Holy fuck."

He collapses on the bed next to me, his shoulders shaking with his breathless laugh. "My thoughts exactly."

That was fast. But intense. Insane. Every time we're together is better than the last. If things keep going in this direction I could actually die of pleasure by the end of the week. "I think I forgot what planet we're on."

His hand snags mine and he drags it up to his mouth, brushing his lips across my knuckles. "We're back on the shitty planet where you're getting dressed to leave this room."

He doesn't sound like he likes the plan. Neither do I, but it's one I made to give him a break from me. And to give me some much needed perspective.

I hate perspective.

"I could text her and tell her to forget it," I offer tentatively. Because screw breathing room. "We don't have to leave this bed at all. Skip the break and go right to where you're spending the night. All night. As much as I can take."

He groans and rolls to his side, pulling me closer and sifting his hands through my hair. "Why do I get the feeling we had a communication glitch? I didn't want you going anywhere, JD. If I had my way… What I mean is, I've been trying not to push you. Trying to restrain myself, because every time you touch me or kiss me, I'm tempted to take too much. You gave me the day, and I wanted it to be about more than sex. I wanted us to spend time together so you'd know how I—"

The faint ringing of my cell phone drifts down the hall, interrupting him. Almost immediately his phone joins in. Both go to voicemail, and then the ringing starts back up again.

"Son of a bitch." He buries his face in my neck and kisses me before heaving himself off of the bed to go find our phones. "Hold that thought."

I have a feeling I might be holding it for a while, and I know it's going to drive me nuts. What was he about to say? And why had he waited until now to say it?

I may never know. Because that ringing sound is real life acting a lot like my editor.

Cock blocker.

***

"JD?"

"Fiona? What are you doing here?" I look up in surprise, opening my arms just in time to accept her embrace. "Hey, what's wrong? Are you okay?"

She leans back to frown at me in consternation. "Am *I* okay? You're the one I followed to the police station, JD. Are *you* okay? Where's Carter?"

"He's still talking to one of the arresting officers. And I'm sorry if my text was confusing. You didn't need to come here. To be honest, I'm not sure we did either."

"What do you mean?"

"I mean I'm icing on the cake, but I don't think I'm the reason our criminal masterminds aren't being granted bail. Toni is."

Fiona, who was glancing down the hall behind her, whipped her head back in my direction. "Your neighbor? Oh hell, what did he do to her?"

"Nothing. No, he didn't—she's fine," I say reassuringly, running my hands through my hair. "She didn't go with him, Fiona. She sent him to prison instead."

"You look pale, JD. Do you need to sit down? Tell me what you're talking about."

Maybe I should sit. I'm still reeling. Carter and I raced to the station after we got the call that Brent and Eddie had been brought in. A few minutes after we'd arrived I discovered Toni was there, specifically waiting to talk to me, I wasn't sure how to respond.

After everything she said, I'm still not.

I follow Fiona to a row of black, plastic chairs attached to the wall and sit down next to her. "She'd arranged to speak to me before we got here. They put us in a private room and she just started talking."

"What did she say?"

"That she saw Eddie's car parked down the street a few hours before my date and she'd panicked, thinking he'd finally come after her. "

"Where did she go that night?" Fiona asked scowling. "And why didn't she warn you about that asshole?"

"She wanted to." I lean my head against the wall, still trying to take it all in. "All I got was the basics. She had a safe deposit box with a SIM card and a flash drive that linked Eddie, Brent and a few others to some serious crime. Serious enough that I'm feeling lucky all they did was stab my couch. It was her push-button-in-case-of-emergency option, and she decided to contact the DEA and use it. That's where she went that night. Since then, they've been watching out for her until the police could make an arrest."

"Wow. Okay, that sounds like it would make a great movie of the week, but you still haven't told me why she let you go on that date."

"I thought Brent was telling the truth. That he'd broken off with Eddie like I did, and he wanted the same second chance. He admitted he was gay and that he'd been in love with Eddie for years. He cried in my arms all night, JD. It didn't feel like a lie. A few days later, when he said he wished he could find someone like you, I thought maybe you could help him. Show him it was ok to be himself...I don't know.

197

When I found out it was a lie, I didn't know what to do. I was worried they would hurt you if you didn't *go. If you were home and tried to protect me. When I heard you'd been...I wanted to come back and take care of you, but the agents told me to stay out of sight until Eddie was caught. I swear to you, if I'd had any idea what they'd planned, I would have stopped you from going. I would have told you everything."*

But she didn't. She ensured her ex and his friend would do actual time and that she would be safe. I was genuinely grateful for both those things. But in her survival-induced panic, she didn't think everything through. She didn't stop me from stepping into the middle of her sting, unprepared. She didn't call me so I could stop agonizing over her safety and feeling guilty for not doing more to help her.

"She had her reasons," is all I can say. "The point is it's over now."

Fiona looks pissed. "Are you kidding me, JD? *She had her reasons?* I can't decide if I want to applaud her balls or bitch slap her into the middle of next week for what she put you through."

That makes me smile. Carter basically said the same

thing. He was furious. He hadn't been willing to look at her when she left with the hovering DEA agent.

But looking back, she did try to warn me, as much as she thought she safely could. She told me not to go home with him. Not to ride in his car. As scared as she must have been, there was still a part of her that was worried about me. That's something.

Fiona glances over her shoulder again.

"What's going on?" I ask. "Who are you looking for?"

Now she looks guilty. "What, Fiona? Spill."

She fiddles with her piercing nervously. "I wasn't sure where to bring them. I was taking them to the bookstore but then you messaged me that you were coming here so—"

"Bring who? Are you talking about Wyatt and that Thor guy?"

She throws me a glare. "Like I need your help to deal with that. I'm screwing it up just great on my own, thanks."

That didn't sound good. "Then who?"

"Your father and brother."

"*What*?" I can actually feel the blood draining from my face. "Rick's here? Not home in Washington where he lives but… Which brother?" There's only one it can be. "Big irritating Samoan guy?"

She nods and I curse under my breath. "He promised he wouldn't tell them."

Royal and Rick are here. And so is Carter. My worlds are about to collide in a police station and it's giving me one hell of a headache. *Not right now. Not after Toni and…*

I'd been having a great day until that damn phone rang.

The phone.

"Was *that* what the all caps is about? Why didn't you say anything in your texts? *Hey there, your dad says hi.* Something like that. And how did they end up with you?"

She shrugs helplessly. "They went to your apartment and your landlord told them the name of the bar. He also mentioned that the last time he'd seen you, some angry, older guy you'd met at Finn's was following you around."

"Seriously? Jesus." Someone clearly didn't like Carter telling him what to do.

"I was there for early deliveries and I heard them talking to Thoreau, describing you and asking questions.

So I introduced myself and the next thing I know, I'm driving them around town, taking them to lunch and trying to avoid them showing up on Carter's doorstep, looking for you."

"Thank you. I owe you. *A lot* of favors." Especially considering what we were doing before we left the house. "Did they say anything about why they'd come without calling me?"

"If we'd called you first, son, you would have told us you were fine. Even if the world was on fire."

I hear his voice and despite my panic, I smile. "Hey, Rick."

No taller than Fiona and more round than he used to be, my foster father is wearing his favorite bowling shirt and that familiar weathered grin as he greets me. "This lovely lady tells me you've been staying with a strange man during your recovery."

We don't beat around the bush in my family.

"Friend," Fiona interjects, a shocked laugh escaping her lips. "You know I only said friend."

Royal towers over Rick, pats the man's baldhead teasingly and throws me a wink. "I think strange man sounds more realistic. Or we could go with the landlord's description. *Angry, older man*. Either way, we were surprised. We didn't think you had any friends."

"Never not funny," I say faintly. I can't believe they're here.

He charges in and hugs me before I have a chance to defend myself. Trapping my arms and lifting me off my feet, I groan a little as he squeezes my ribs.

"Put him down."

Carter.

Why me, Lord?

I let out a long-suffering sigh when Royal doesn't budge. "Carter, this is Royal. He's a brother. Royal this is Carter. He's a friend."

"Hello friend."

"Hello brother," Carter responds with a pleasant smile and dark, dangerous eyes. "You'll want to go ahead and put him down now. He's still recovering."

"Shit," Royal swears, setting me gently on my feet and straightening my shirt. "Sorry about that, JD. I just… I'm glad you're okay."

I cross my arms, sensing Carter closing in behind me. "Sure. I'm great. I'd be better if you hadn't dragged Rick across the country for absolutely no reason. Do you remember our conversation the other night? The one where you swore you would keep what happened to yourself, because I'd never hear the end of it?"

Royal holds up a correcting hand. "I never said that. Check the transcripts. You *asked me* not to tell anyone and I *avoided* responding directly. All I remember definitely agreeing to was not to bring Dickie and Manwich along to crack any skulls."

Rick chuckles. "You know Matilda hates it when you call them that."

"I know," Royal says, lifting his gaze to stare at Carter with brotherly intimidation. "So. You're angry, old and strange."

"Excuse me?"

Before I can explain or kick Royal in the shin, my foster father chimes in. "You're the *friend* who stopped two men from attacking JD? The one Fiona and the landlord both swear is responsible for not letting him stay at his apartment by himself after it was broken into?"

Royal shoots a scowl in my direction. "FYI, I don't remember getting that part of the story."

"FYI, nobody says FYI anymore." I'm tempted to stick out my tongue, but I'm an adult now. I don't do things like that now. In public.

"I'm Carter Willis. And you must be Rick." Carter

sets his hands on my shoulders and I tense, too aware of everyone's interest at the move. "To answer your question, yes, he's been staying with me."

"Just until I get my locks changed," I blurt, worried Royal will say something about sugar daddies and I'll end up being arrested for assault. "He's a security guy so… And it's huge. His house."

Fiona sends me a look that says, *"What the hell just came out of your mouth?"*

I respond with, *"You brought them here. And have you met me?"*

Rick, who's used to my filterless foot-in-mouth issues, ignores us both in favor of studying Carter. "Jimmy has never been good at accepting help. He always wanted to take care of things on his own and in his own way. It's the reason we had to hide the bleach on laundry day and call his teachers on a regular basis to find out if we'd signed any permission slips we weren't aware of. And he hated anyone knowing when he was hurt or sick. You wouldn't believe the subterfuge Matilda and I were reduced to just to find out whether or not the stubborn boy had a fever."

That's what he's leading with? Why is he telling Carter about my childhood quirks?

Royal chuckles. "Remember when we cleaned out the freezer and found all those thermometers stuck to the back?"

I glare and he crosses his arms in irritation. "They kept buying new ones. It was funny as hell."

"He hasn't changed all that much." Carter's hands squeeze my shoulders supportively, but I can hear his amusement. "I had to bribe him with homemade barbecue sauce to leave his apartment."

Rick's eyes widen, and then he's laughing. So hard he has to lean against a shocked Royal when his mirth nearly bends him in half. "I…I had to use…books."

I'm not sure what they're talking about. "Nothing is that funny."

But Fiona is laughing at me too. "So cute," she chortles. "I will never get over how cute you are. Or, apparently, how reward motivated. No wonder you gave me that carrot advice. But we can talk about that later."

"We're in a police station," I say, loud enough to be heard over the hilarity.

Rick wipes his eyes, nodding. "Yes, I know. But I only know *why* you're in a police station because Royal called Joey yesterday to ask his advice. He happened to be having lunch with me at the time, so I overheard and took the next flight out." He looks into my eyes, humor gone. "I decided to find out what was really going on before I mentioned it to Matilda."

Which explains why she isn't here with reporters and her interns in tow. "I understand. I'm sorry you were worried, but Matilda definitely doesn't need to be. I was telling Fiona that the men have already been arrested. Not just for—"

"JD Green." Rick was using his disappointed professor voice. *Shit.* "If you believe she'd want to know about anything other than your well-being, then you don't know who raised you." I open my mouth and he *shushes* me. "And if you say you're fine I won't be held responsible for my actions."

I bite my lip because that was exactly what I was going to say. I'm surprised at how upset he is. Rick survived years of childhood tantrums all while smiling and appearing utterly relaxed. I still think he had a weed stash somewhere in the garage, because no man with ten boys could be that chill all the time.

"Do the two of you have a place to stay, sir?" Carter asks respectfully.

Royal smirks "Why? Before you answer, I have a list of favorite foods you can bribe me with."

Rick gives him a look that shuts him down. "We're staying in a suite near the airport. And please, call me Rick."

He takes Fiona's hand in his. "My dear, we appreciate your help in locating my lost sheep of a son. Would you like to join us for dinner?"

"I'd love to." She notices my bulging eyes and winks. "Unfortunately, I have to work tonight. But if you feel like stopping by for drinks and gossiping about what JD was like as a child *after* dinner, they'll be on the house."

Rick gives her a solemn smile. "We'll take it under consideration."

He glances at Carter. "Royal ordered a car for us before we came in. You and JD can follow us back to the hotel. There's a restaurant in the lobby where we can talk."

"We'll be right behind you."

We. One word melts the knots in my stomach and makes my headache disappear like magic.

I look over at Royal. "The paperwork is done here, but I want to make sure they don't need me for anything else. Text me the address and we'll meet you there."

Rick surprises me again by pulling me in for a hard hug. "I'm glad you're okay, Jimmy."

I close my eyes and breathe in the familiar, comforting scent of old books and cedar. "I'm glad you're here, Rick."

He pats my back and steps away, blinking rapidly. "I'm starving, so don't keep us waiting long. Oh, and I found my old, signed copy of *A Short History of Nearly Everything*. It's in my luggage if you'd like to refresh your memory."

I have a Pavlovian response to this information, but now that they've joked about using my weaknesses against me, I'm trying not to be obvious. "I'm glad you finally found it. But you know it's full of errors now."

"We can discuss Pluto over dinner, Jimmy."

Royal snorts and then the two of them, along with a grinning Fiona, say their goodbyes and disappear together down the hall.

When they're gone, I finally turn to face Carter. His expression is difficult to read. What else is new? "Busy day. First I bring you to the police station for hours of excitement, and now this unexpected twist. If it's too *Meet the Parents*, you can say no."

He gathers the hem of my shirt in his fist and tugs me closer, until every part of me that can be pressed against him is. Oh. "Or we could both skip it. Your call."

"We're going to dinner, Green. But I'm not letting you out of my sight. I have a feeling if I do, they'll grab you and sneak you out of town."

I laugh. "That's the last thing you have to worry about. I'm surprised they're here at all. It's the middle of the semester for Rick and I already told Royal I was fine."

He shakes his head, his expression almost perplexed. "You don't see it."

"See what?"

Carter grips my shoulders and physically turns me towards the parking lot. "I'll tell you when I get you back home. And we're naked."

"Bribery again?"

"I heard you were reward motivated. I'll use whatever works."

CHAPTER NINE

"If Rick weren't six years older than your boyfriend, I think he'd try to adopt him," Royal says as we watch the two of them having an animated conversation at a table in the hotel lounge.

"Shut up." He's my brother. I don't have to expand on that.

He's not wrong. Rick and Carter are getting along as if they've known each other all their lives. The absentminded professor and the drill instructor. I can see it. They both spent their careers shaping young minds. They're both interested in history. Too interested. By the time we'd wandered from the restaurant to the lounge, they were having an in-depth discussion on historical battle strategies.

I can't contribute, but I won't try to put a stop to it either. It means they aren't talking about me.

Royal managed to escape to the bar to flirt with the bartender. He's only talking to me now because I'm ordering another round of drinks.

"Why did you call Joey?" I ask him after giving her our order.

Royal leans his elbows on the bar and shrugs. "He deals with kids all the time, and you were acting like one. It made sense."

I whack his arm and try not to flinch when it hurts my hand. He gives me his signature cocky grin. "See what I mean?" I wait him out with a blank expression. "Fine. I called him because I was worried about you, and he's the only one you ever talked to about your problems."

I frown. "That's not true. He was always too busy working to talk to me." That and Joey is only serious when it's business related. In his personal life, he's like a giant kid. Luckily, he can afford the best toys.

I guess that's another thing Joey, Royal and I all have in common. We aren't big fans of adulting.

"Then who *did* you talk to? I know it wasn't me."

I sigh. "You seem to be forgetting how weird and

socially awkward I was. I avoided talking to all of you equally. About my problems anyway. You, however, are the only brother on my emergency contact list."

He smiles and pats my back. "Good point. You *were* pretty weird. But useful. My little human lie detector."

That nickname brings back memories. "I still wish you hadn't come all this way for nothing. Or that you'd called me before abducting Fiona so I could tell you where I was."

"That's another thing." Royal's big shoulders bunch when he reaches for a bowl of stale pretzels on the counter, popping a handful into his mouth. "What's going on with that? You meet this guy, and a few hours later you're staying at his house while he *nurses you back to health*. And you seem good with it. Hell, you're glowing." He points at me. "You. The guy who wouldn't ask for a ride in a thunderstorm. The guy who is so picky about men we have six months of reading material on you *not* getting to first base. Is Mr. Dry Spell suddenly Mr. Relationship?"

I grit my teeth as heat fills my cheeks. "Are you reading my diary?"

He snorts again. "It's online, genius. Don't kid yourself. We're all reading it."

Logically, I know that. But I try not to think about what that means when it comes to my family. "I wouldn't say Carter nursed me back to health. I told you already, it wasn't that bad. All he did was help me out when—"

"You're into him. Admit it."

"I'm admitting nothing."

"You don't have to." Royal tapped a finger to his temple. "I don't need your skills to figure this one out. I know *you*. And you are totally getting some of that kinky, older man action."

He's smiling so broadly I almost have to tell him, even if he is a giant pain in the ass. "I won't say you're right. But you're not wrong."

"*I knew it*. Man. Never thought I'd see the day JD Green fell in love."

The bartender smiles as she brings me our drink tray and I lower my voice. "Did I say that, Royal? I didn't and I'm not going to because that would be *crazy*. I've only known him for a couple of days. He's only known me when my life is a total disaster."

Royal is ignoring me in favor of eyeing the bartender. "Some people only need forty-five minutes to know for sure. Isn't that right, Alicia?"

Her eyes sparkle as she takes in Royal's broad shoulders. Everything about her body language says she agrees. "I'll let you know. We still have five minutes left."

"I'll leave you to it." I try not to roll my eyes as I balance the tray.

Royal puts his hand on my shoulder. "I'm sorry if we crossed the line by showing up uninvited. And however you feel about him, I'm glad you at least think he's someone you can trust."

"You didn't cross any line, Royal. We're family. I was surprised, that's all."

Surprised and guilty, because Royal had been worried enough to call in backup. The last thing I wanted was anyone worrying over me.

We've only spoken a handful of times in the last few years, but he's still looking out for me. In between his teasing, I know he always tried to. I'm just… me. Bad at asking for help, apparently. That seems to be the running theme for tonight. As subtle as a hammer.

JD is a stubborn ass.

Yes, but an ass that isn't in love with a guy he just met last weekend…in a bar.

Stubborn. Ass.

I'm talking to myself. Great.

"There you are!" Rick sounds jovial, his cheeks are flushed and his smile is wider than usual. He and Matilda aren't big drinkers. "I was trying to pry information out of Carter, but I ended up telling him about the rest of your brothers instead."

"He doesn't like to talk about himself. It took me an hour just to find out his name."

"Not a whole hour." Carter accepts his drink, reaching for my hand to tug me into the booth beside him. "And Rick's ten sons are way more interesting. I'm trying to keep up in case there's a test later."

"There might be."

He laughs. "Then let's review. I've met Royal. Craig's given you grandchildren. Then there's Grant the lawyer and Chris the piano teacher. You won't tell me what Dickie and Manwich do for—"

"Hah!" Rick sets his drink down and slaps the table. "Manwich."

I can't help but smile. "No one knows what those two are up to. Well, maybe Royal. But that's a secret he *can* keep."

Carter slips his arm around my shoulders and I lean into his heat gratefully. "Who's left? Stewart is into

215

camping. And Isaac, right? I think Rick told me he lives on an island."

"The surfing ambassador," I offer under my breath.

"And Joey is the babysitter. That's nine."

"He's the most successful child you have, his company is worth millions, and you still introduce him as the babysitter."

"Well he used to be one, and now his company is full of them."

"His. Company," I emphasize.

"Of people trained to look after children. Also known as babysitters," Rick volleys back, his blue eyes sparkling.

"And ten is the barbecue sauce loving, textbook-collecting advice columnist," Carter finishes smoothly, smiling at both of us. "Quite a list. You and your wife must be proud."

I take a large gulp of my rum and coke, unwilling to experience this evening on the hotel's shitty beer. "You've done it now," I whisper loudly.

Rick is already shaking his head. "Matilda and I never believed in taking ownership of their success. Are we impressed? Absolutely. Pride implies we had something to do with it."

"Didn't you? You gave them shelter. Compassion. Education. Authority figures to teach them about life and keep them on the right path."

"You've described most federal institutions. Prisons, for example. Though I think their cooking would be an improvement over mine." He chuckles to himself. "It's the individual that chooses to succeed or fail within the institution, not the institution itself."

I put my hand on Carter's leg and squeeze. "I can't argue with that, Rick. You're one of the most brilliant men I know, but you should never attempt food preparation of any kind."

"Says the boy who set the kitchen on fire."

"Only once."

We laugh but when his eyes meet mine, his smile slowly disappears. "You should have told us what happened, Jimmy."

"I'm sorry." I reach across the table and impulsively take his hand. "I am. But it was only a scuffle, Rick. A black eye. It was more embarrassing than anything. I'm fine, I promise."

"We always enjoyed your independent streak. Maybe too much. I think we should have given you more rules."

"We'll have to disagree on that," I say, trying to tease

another smile out of him. "And I'd bet all the guys would be on my side."

"Parents make rules to protect their children," he says stubbornly, looking down at his drink. "Statistically, a child raised in a structured environment feels more secure."

I glance over at Carter in apology. "Does Matilda know you're reading childrearing books again? Or is there something you wanted to tell me? I thought we'd decided you two weren't bringing anymore kids into the house."

Rick finishes his drink and meets my gaze. "I was trying to understand why you don't feel like you can talk to us about your problems."

Help. "What problems?"

"I saw your apartment. I had no idea you were living like that."

"Now you sound like a snob." I really don't want to have this conversation in front of Carter. "My apartment is perfectly fine. Can we talk about something else? Please?"

"We had the money to send you to college. Everyone else took us up on it, but you wanted to do it on your own. That money is still yours. You could use it on an apartment that's harder to break into and bigger than a closet, and in four years you'll have—" He cuts himself off and shakes his head. "You keep saying you're fine. You know I hate that. Your father said the same thing the day before he died. We believed him and then... I'm fine," he chokes. "Worst two words in the English language."

"Okay." I signal to Royal to wrap it up with the bartender and pat Rick's hand. "I think it might be time to call it a night."

Carter is a quiet presence beside me, and I'm thankful for it, though I wish he wasn't seeing this.

"Hey, Papa Smurf." Royal easily lifts Rick to his feet. "Look at you. Would you mind if I take a video for the rest of the family? You haven't been this toasty since we all turned sixteen."

"Hard year." Rick's chuckle is watery, and he still looks too sad. Luckily, their room is an elevator away.

Royal looks at me in question and I shake my head. "What time are you two heading out?"

"Early."

I push the button to call their ride. Rick sways and reaches for my shirt. "Are you sure you're okay?"

"*You* made sure of it," I tell him firmly. "And I have

friends taking care of me now, so you don't have to worry. I'm not alone."

"I'll still worry." He cups the back of my head and presses our foreheads together. "I think we did it wrong, Jimmy. You were young but we should have told you about—"

"Rick, I'm happy." *You're breaking my heart.* "I promise, you didn't do anything wrong. Not for any of us. And Royal is here now. You go with him and he'll get you to your room, okay?"

I'm hoping he understands that we're not alone so he doesn't say something he'll regret in the morning.

The doors open and I kiss his forehead, handing our silent foster father over to my worried brother. "He's fine," I tell him softly. "He's thinking about my parents."

I'm still staring at the elevator when Carter takes my hand. "Are you going to tell me a story on the way home, JD?"

I look down at our entwined fingers and nod.

"Then let's go."

"What happened with Rick?" Carter asks after we've been on the road for several minutes and I still haven't said a word. "Talk to me."

I look away from the oncoming headlights to study his profile. "I'm sorry about that. I can count on one hand the number of times I've seen Rick drink. When he does, he can get sentimental, though he doesn't usually lecture us on lifestyle choices."

Randomly, I'm thinking I wish I'd had a chance to *clean* my apartment before he'd seen it today.

"What did he mean about your father? What happened to him?"

I take a steadying breath. "He committed suicide."

"Shit." Carter bites off another curse and I watch his strained expression as he searches for a place to pull off and park. As soon as he shuts off the truck and unbuckles his seatbelt, he turns to take my hand. "Do you want to wait to talk about this until we get home?"

I don't want to talk about it at all, and the attention is making me uncomfortable. "You didn't need to pull over, Carter. It's okay. My biological parents are strangers. I only know their names and what they looked like because Matilda made a photo album. But that's all they are to me. Gary and Lauren Green. High school friends of the people who raised me."

When I say that I feel like a bad person. "According

to Matilda my mother was sweet and always smiling. And after I was born, every thought she had was about my future."

Carter's fingers tighten on mine. "And your father?"

"Gary was another story. He'd struggled with depression all his life. I know he loved my mother and his friends, but Rick said there were times he'd disappear or withdraw. Only for a few weeks and then he'd be back as if it never happened. Then his brother died, followed two years later by his wife getting sick. Five days after she was gone, and two weeks before my fourth birthday, he bought a gun."

"Jesus," Carter breathes, leaning his head against the seat beside him.

I've never said it out loud before. "In the note he left, he actually mentioned Kurt Cobain. After losing his wife, his brother and his hero, he said, there was nothing left to live for. *No one* left to live for. I only know about that because Rick still has it in a box in the back of his closet, and once I saw him crying over it."

Carter looks so wrecked I feel bad for telling him. "Not as upbeat as my last story. Sorry about that. The afternoon sort of went to hell, didn't it?"

"I'm glad you told me." He cups my face in his

hands, his thumbs caressing my cheeks. "I mean it, JD. Thank you."

I lean into his touch instinctively. "My brothers don't know. Not the details anyway."

"Why?"

"I didn't want to tell them." I reach up and grip his wrists, needing to touch him. "They all had rough lives before they came to live with us. They deserved a fresh start in a good home."

"Are you saying you didn't?"

"No. But I never struggled like they did. Rick and Matilda took me in before I even went into the system. I was lucky but…"

"But what?"

"You saw Rick tonight. I'm a constant reminder of a painful memory. You know, they didn't plan on having kids? Sometimes I think they felt so guilty for not noticing their friend was suicidal that they atoned the only way they knew how. By making sure I didn't end up like him."

His hands drop to my shoulders in a painful grip and gives me a little shake that startles me. "JD, that's…" He fades off, incredulous. "It's wrong. Completely wrong. I don't claim to know what their initial reasons were, but that man's actions today spoke loud and clear. He flew across the country to let you know he cared and wants to be more involved in your life. As far as he's concerned, you're his son."

"I know it. And I know how lucky I am that Rick raised me. We all are. He's a good man."

"So are you." Carter is massaging my shoulders, trying to work the tension away. "But for someone so skilled at observation, there are one or two things you refuse to see."

"Like what?"

"How special you are."

"Carter, I'm not—"

"I didn't say perfect," he interrupts. "But I've seen how you look at people, into people and know exactly what they need to hear, the way you did with Wyatt and Rick. I've seen the way you can find the humor in any situation, and how you share it to help other people find a little happiness in this world. That's who *you* are. What you *do*. And if I can see it after a few days of being around you, I have no doubt your family already knows and loves that about you. You're not an obligation, JD. You're a gift."

Before I can second guess myself I'm straddling his

hips and kissing him like it's been months instead of a few hours since I tasted his lips and tangled with his tongue.

I love his mouth. I love how his words make me feel. Admired. Seen.

I love the way he sees me.

Carter groans and digs his fingers into my hips, pulling me onto the erection already trying to tear its way through his jeans. "We can't…not here….*JD*."

Right here. I unbutton my pants and look through the windows at the dark lot outside, before twisting around to reach beneath my seat for the plastic bag I'd discovered earlier. "I saw this on the drive to the station. You must have had big plans for tonight, Zeus."

A large box of condoms and two bottles of lube pour onto the passenger seat and Carter's hands slide up to my waist. "You know I have plans. Let me get you home and show you, JD. Where I can take care of you. Where I have room to touch you. Make you come."

"We were interrupted," I tell him as I move to kneel beside him, pulling off my shirt and pushing my jeans and underwear impatiently down to my thighs. "We were having a great day, and then it all went downhill. I need to forget everything else and get back to that."

225

I open one of the bottles and meet his gaze. "So take care of me."

The thick liquid coats the tips of my fingers and I reach behind me, rubbing it into the skin I want him to touch. Then I take his hand, and guide it to the curve of my ass. "Touch me."

When he starts to stroke and squeeze I bend over, open his belt and take his erection out with shaking fingers.

"Make me come."

CHAPTER TEN

"Jesus Fucking—"

I take the hard length of him in my mouth with an appreciative hum, and the second his taste bursts on my tongue I want more of it. More of him.

Everything.

Carter swears softly and slips one hand into my loose hair, holding it away from my face so he can see what I'm doing. At the same time, I feel his thick fingers rubbing and pressing against me, relaxing the tight muscles until I'm opening for him and he's filling me up. *Yes.*

"I thought I told you I didn't want anyone else to see you like this," he rasps, tugging my hair in sensual warning. "Now your sweet, sexy ass is bare. Anyone driving by could see it naked and open for me, begging to be spanked. Fucked."

I moan with arousal. I love it when he talks like that. His gravelly voice soaked in sin. *Spank me. Fuck me. Anything you want.*

"Is this what you want, baby?" he croons, slipping out long enough to land a warm smack on the center of my ass. When he thrusts his fingers back inside, a third is forcing its way inside my tight hole. I whimper but push back into it, craving more.

"That's right, take what you need. You're beautiful, like this. Filled front and back and taking everything I give you. Is it too much? Can you open your mouth wider? Take a little more?"

I stretch my lips wide and breathe out, relaxing against him. Giving him control so he can take what he wants.

"Jesus, that's perfect. You're so damn perfect. You make it hard to hold back."

Don't hold back.

There's no way I can take all of him, but he doesn't try to make me. Instead, his hand in my hair guides me up and down his shaft in a slow, careful rhythm. Too slow. Too careful.

I tease and explore every inch I can reach with my tongue, paying extra attention to the head of his cock, greedy for the hot, salty taste of him.

"You're trying to make me come," he mutters darkly. "But I'm not ready for this to be over yet. You started this, so you can let me set the pace."

I want to challenge him, to make him as impatient as I am, but his fingers keep distracting me. Spreading and thrusting, filling me while avoiding the spot I need them most. I lift my ass higher in silent demand.

Carter's laugh has an edge like nails dragging up my spine. "Stop being so impatient, JD. I need to see if you're ready to take my cock."

My muffled shout is loud in the cramped space when a fourth finger works its way inside me. I can't. It's too much. He caresses my head gently when I tense against him.

"Breathe, JD. Breathe and relax for me."

So full. I'm shaking my head and moaning, the sound vibrating along his cock and making him swear.

"You can take it," he's murmuring. "And when I get you home, you'll take all of me, won't you?"

Yes. That's what I want.

But right now, all I can think about is making him

come. I want to shatter his control the way he always shatters mine.

With his hand still caressing my head, I lean forward before he knows what I'm up to, swallowing him so deeply I choke, but I don't stop until I feel his shuddering reaction. "Fuck, JD."

His grip on my hair tightens again as I suck mercilessly on his hot, hard shaft and he thrusts his hips up in helpless response. "Fuck. Fuck. *Fuck*."

Yes. Yes. Yes.

His release hits the back of my throat in powerful spurts and I shiver with pleasure, knowing I did that. I made him lose control. He wants me that much.

I close my eyes and inhale his scent, the taste of him, hoarding every sensation.

"You definitely need a spanking," he huffs out when he finally catches his breath.

I feel almost empty when he takes his fingers away to reach in the bag for a small package of sanitizing wipes, cleaning us both in swift, efficient silence.

My head is on his thigh and I force myself to keep still, waiting for him to touch me. To turn me around and fuck me. I'm so ready to come.

My eyes open wide at the sound of the truck's

engine.

"Carter?"

"You stay right there," he growls. "Don't sit up, don't move until I get you home."

He holds my head against his thigh with one hand, the other on the wheel as he speeds down the road.

"Can I at least pull my pants up?"

"No."

I glance over at the damp cock nestled in his still-open jeans and bite my lip. He's already getting hard again. My ass clenches in response. Tonight, he said. He'd take me the way he wanted to tonight.

Thinking about it, all the things he could do to me, all the positions I've imagined, has my hand lowering to my erection by the time he turns into his driveway.

"No touching. I mean it, JD." He moves my hand away and turns off the ignition, opening the door.

I start to sit up, but he's dragging me toward him and moving me around like I'm a doll instead of grown man. He slips off my shoes and takes my jeans completely off before tossing them in the truck's cab. "Wrap your legs around my waist."

"I hope your neighbors aren't looking out the window," I mumble, naked and clinging to him as he grabs his bag of supplies and carries me into the house.

"You should have thought of that before you decided to strip in my truck." He kicks the door shut behind us and heads straight for his bedroom. "Next time you'll know better."

Bossy, controlling, fucking sexy… "You seemed to like it. At least you got to come."

"You'll get your chance as soon as I'm where I belong."

He tosses me onto his bed and all of a sudden, I'm having trouble breathing. "Oh."

"Hands above your head and keep them there." He barks the command. He's undressing, his dark eyes pinning me to his giant bed as effectively as restraints.

I stretch for him, letting him see everything. Wanting him to look. I can't remember ever being this turned on by someone watching me. This needy and shameless.

"I'll never get enough of that view."

He rips open the box of condoms and slides one on with swift, expert movements. He coats it with lube, tossing the bottle nearby and crawling on the bed beside me. His expression is fierce. Unstoppable.

Big Daddy Zeus.

I gasp when he spreads my legs and ignores my

erection in favor of my ass. His fingers part my cheeks and he lowers his head without hesitation, licking and sucking and tonguing me until I'm close to tears.

"Carter, please." I feel jittery. Panicked and out of control. "Oh God."

I don't want him to stop.

He bites into the flesh of my ass and growls. "I had plans for this ass," he rasps. "For every part of you. Hours of plans, grasshopper."

His tongue traces the birthmark on my hip. "I wanted to learn every curve and bend of this beautiful body. Find every freckle with my tongue."

"Sounds like torture," I manage to form the words between moans.

"The kind that would have you begging. And we both know how much I like hearing you beg."

I hold my breath when his lips barely skim my cock. *Please.* "But those plans have to wait, because I can't anymore. I have to get inside you."

Thank God.

He leans over me, guiding my legs up over his shoulders and holding both my wrists in one snug fist.

"Are you going to give me what I want, JD?" he asks, reminding me of that night in his kitchen, and the fantasy that followed.

It feels like I've been waiting forever to give him his answer.

"Yes, Carter."

He kisses me, pressing against the back of my legs until my hips are in the air and my knees are pushing against my shoulders. I can feel precum coating my stomach and every beat of my heart is pulsing through my dick. "Please," I moan against his mouth. "I'm begging you."

He lifts his head, breathing heavily as he looks into my eyes. I feel the wide head of his cock slide inside and watch as he closes his eyes and his strong body visibly quakes.

"Fuck, JD." My name comes out on a growl and then his eyes are open and I'm trapped again, seeing the need there that mirrors mine. Seeing something I'm too afraid to name.

The way he's pinning me makes it impossible to move or test his hold. Impossible to touch or tease him. I'm open and vulnerable and all I can do is take. "*Please*."

"I've got you," he says, his hips thrusting forward slow enough that I can feel every thick, impossible inch of his cock spreading me wide. It's too much. Too good.

I start to shake against him.

"A little more," he says roughly. "Just a little more, baby."

I follow his gaze to see him filling me. His beast of a cock is splitting me open, disappearing inside me. Making me his.

My moan comes out more like a sob, and I can't look away. "*Zeus*."

"JD, look at me." I blink up at him, dazed and so full I'm not sure I have room to take another breath. "This is where I belong," he rasps. "Can you feel it? I need to…"

He shifts his hips and I cry out when his dick grinds against my prostate. "Fuck."

The tendons in his neck are tight and his teeth are bared as he lowers his head until our lips are inches apart. "I knew the second I saw your face that you'd own me."

Me? He's the one controlling everything. The one I'd do anything to— *Oh God, I can't think.*

He starts to move. Small, shallow pulses at first, until my body relaxes around him. Then long steady strokes that drive us both to the brink, before he slows again. Pulling us back. He's keeping me guessing, keeping me hanging, and all the while he's staring into my eyes, breathing with me. Breathing for me.

This is more than sex. More than fucking.

Zeus is worshipping me.

He plays with my body, his free hand caressing my throat, skimming my nipples. He's reacting to every moan and cry, discovering what I like. What I need. How long he can make me wait. "I've got you, baby."

"You know where I need you to touch me," I plead raggedly. Just one touch and I can come. I'm close. "I'm dying."

"Not yet." His body is glistening with heat and restraint. "This feels too good. Exactly right. Goldilocks Zone, remember?"

"*Carter, please.*"

He groans, his thrusts growing more forceful. "Love it when you beg."

"Please, let me come, Carter. Fuck me harder. Don't stop. I need you."

With a wild moan, he lets go, giving me what I want. Hard and deep. His body straining over mine.

Yes.

"Such a good boy. Love fucking you. Let me… *Christ*!"

Good boy. That's all it takes for me to come without a single stroke of my cock. I've been so close for so long, but it still surprises me, crashing into me with the force of a wrecking ball. My channel spasms around him, making the tight fit almost painful and Carter shouts again.

I can't stop it. I don't want to. I can't do anything but let my release wash over me, sending rough tremors up my spine and soaking my stomach with come as Carter loses all restraint.

"*So good*," he moans. He's fucking me so hard now, the sound of his flesh slapping against mine like erotic applause.

He grips my jaw with his free hand and kisses me. Then he jerks up, his eyes clenched shut as he comes with a long, hoarse shout. I can feel the heat of his release through the condom, pulsing inside me.

This is bliss. This is what people are willing to do anything to feel. To keep.

What they'd die without.

I feel like I lost time or left my body for a few minutes, and it's almost impossible to keep a thought in my head.

I've never felt so out of control.

Carter drags me close and pulls the sheet over our cooling bodies.

"Still with me?" He murmurs, kissing my neck and using his knuckles to brush the tears off my cheeks. "JD?"

"What planet again?"

His chuckle is low and intimate. "Our planet, grasshopper. And let me tell you, I really like it here. I don't plan on leaving anytime soon."

I don't just like it here. I love it here.

I love…

Three hours later, I'm climbing into a car that's going to take me to the airport and my brother's plane.

I left a note for Carter.

Spending a few days with family. Thank you for everything. Will talk to you soon.

Soon. This is a break. Breathing room. Everyone needs some space now and then.

I need a little distance. Hopefully there'll be enough of it to convince myself I'm not hopelessly in love for the first time in my life.

Because I can't be.

That can't be what I'm feeling, right?

Dear Diary,

I...fuck, I can't talk about it right now.

***

9 days later…

"Good morning, sunshine. I don't mean to interrupt this ode to moping you've been working on, but I was wondering if you were planning on taking a shower ever again. I've been gone for three days and you're still exactly where I left you. In the same clothes, with that same appetizing stain on your collar."

I flip Royal off without looking away from the view. This apartment is perfect for him. Playboy pilot bachelor digs done right, but it's got nothing on his balcony. I've barely left it in the last nine days.

Nine. Days.

He's right. I'm in the same clothes I was in when he left for work a few days ago. I haven't moved in so long that the pigeons that drop by for lunch think I'm one of their own. The fat one with a chip in his beak is my spirit animal.

Chip gets me.

Despite my lack of welcome, Royal grabs a chair and

takes a seat. Great. I thought we were beyond the talking thing, but it's not like I can kick him out. I pick up a half empty container of chunky liquid and grimace. Old, melted Moose Tracks. Yum. "What's up?"

"Thanks for asking, JD. There's actually a lot going on in my life right now. My brother hit and quit a Marine, then holed up in my apartment to hide from the world. Not that I mind a visit every now and then," he amends with a shrug. "But this kind of behavior is just begging for an intervention, and those sound like too much work, so I'm naturally against them."

"Do you want me to leave?"

"Don't be a dick," he says sharply. "I want you to snap out of it. This isn't like you."

How does he know? Maybe it is. Maybe I don't deserve to snap out of it.

I left the best man I'd ever known after the best sex I'd ever had because I was scared of what *might* happen. How fucked up is that? I was scared of being in love with someone who might not feel the same, or as much as I did. So in love that losing him would… well, it would do this to me.

I thought it might get better. That the feeling might pass with time and distance. Perspective and logic was all I needed. But I was wrong. If anything it's gotten worse.

I can't stop thinking about him. I can't write. I can't help feeling I made a horrible mistake.

Fiona thinks so too. She's calling me every day, checking in on me and repeating the same words of comfort. "Stop being an idiot."

She might be my best friend.

Toni contacted me a few days ago, apologizing via email, but after what I did to Carter, I don't think I deserve an apology anymore. She may have panicked and made a few horrible decisions, but I'm the real coward. I won't even take the chance of being hurt.

What kind of advice columnist am I? I think it rhymes with hypocrite.

Physician heal thyself.

Is this what depression feels like? Sitting on a balcony in dirty pajamas, trapped in a sluggish time suck of inaction that eats away at your soul until nothing else matters?

Maybe I'm just like my father…

Nope. If my silent self-pity binge can morph into a Prince song that quickly, I haven't quite hit bottom yet. Maybe there's hope.

"Earth to JD."

"It's not that easy to snap out of this, Royal. You don't understand."

"Yes, I do."

"No, you don't."

"But I really do."

"Stop." I run both my hands through my hair and cringe. That feels like it can't be a good look. "Fine. What do you think you know?"

Royal leans forward to look at the skyline. "I know this situation is your own fault and you need to get over it before you screw it up for good. I know some guy named Tanaka is Matilda's new cyber pen pal and...what else? Oh yeah, I know I'm the most attractive brother you have and that right now you smell like cottage cheese."

I whack him out of habit then stare, wide-eyed. "Tanaka? What? With who?"

"Witty. You should write that down." At my glare he holds up his hands. "All I know is he started talking to her last week. Don't ask me how he got her number, but she was impressed. He was worried about his friend, but said that Carter wouldn't give him details beyond the fact that he'd pushed you into talking about your past and scared you away—"

"He didn't push me into anything." But I can't deny I ran. Even now I can't bring myself to listen to any of his messages, afraid of what I'll hear. And he's filled up my voicemail twice. "But why did Tanaka call Matilda?"

And did Carter know about it?

"She and Rick are in the living room now, so I guess you can ask her yourself."

"What?" I stand up so fast I get dizzy and might have tipped off of the balcony if my brother hadn't grabbed hold of my pants. "What are they doing here? Why didn't you tell me?"

"I am telling you." Royal stands beside me, wrinkling his nose. "And they had no choice. I refused to take you to them, because that would require being seen with you in public."

"I get it. I'm gross and I stink. But seriously, tell me why they're here."

He bends to look directly into my eyes. "They. Are. Worried about you," he says slowly and succinctly. "Oh and they said it was time to tell you about your grandparents."

Grandparents? What the fuck?

He uses my shock to fast walk me inside the

apartment and towards the shower, bypassing the living room so no one else has to see or smell me.

After closing the door, I turn on the water and strip, groaning in relief when the hot spray finally starts to work its magic on the first layer of filth.

Tanaka and Matilda? That's a scary combination. The idea of them talking at all is making me nervous. But if he sought her out, it had to be because Carter was suffering. The thought sends an ache through my heart.

He deserves better than this. He's never run away from anything. Not his family, not his duty, not me.

But *why* is he suffering about me? What could he possibly see in me that's worth my childish, neurotic bullshit?

He already told you.

I freeze as the water beats against my thick skull, giving me clarity for the first time in weeks.

Son of a bitch.

He did.

All the behavior I was suspicious of, that I didn't trust is suddenly replaying in my mind. The way he watched out for me. The way he listened. His soft smile when I rambled.

His face when he came inside me.

He's not suffering because he liked having me around for company or ready sex or any of the other asinine reasons I came up with in my addled brain.

He's hurting because he cared and I walked away from him. He's hurting because I won't return his phone calls.

He's hurting because he was falling in love with you.

I turn off the water and let several days' worth of dirt and sadness slide down the drain.

"I am officially the biggest fucking idiot on the planet." I look into the mirror and his loving voice echoes in my head.

Our planet, grasshopper.

"Shit!"

I hear Royal's laugh on the other side of the door. "Are you done having shower epiphanies? Our parents need some handholding while they bare their souls and that's your department. I'm just here to shuttle people around and look pretty."

I get myself together, grab some clothes and join them in the living room, feeling strangely naked without my coating of misery. Still, all I can think about is Carter…until I see Matilda.

Rick is standing next to my swollen-eyed foster

mom. Her dark, mahogany curls are unbound and she isn't wearing makeup. I'm pretty sure I've never seen her without it.

I'm also almost positive I've never seen her cry. "Are you okay? Do you need to sit down?"

She shakes her head. She's holding a thick file against her chest and she's silent until Rick wraps his arm around her waist. As if he pushed a button, she automatically starts talking.

"Rick wanted to tell you years ago, but I put it off. He mentioned it again after his visit, but by then you were already here with Royal. Then Ken…"

She's calling him Ken instead of Tanaka? How much talking did they do? "Matilda, Royal mentioned something about grandparents? Is that what this is about? I thought Gary's parents were dead."

"Your mother's parents," Rick answers when she doesn't speak up. "They're the ones that fought Lauren's will and made sure we couldn't legally adopt you."

I stumble back as if I've been sucker punched, looking up in surprise at Royal when he guides me silently to his leather sofa. "Thanks."

He nods and sits down beside me, close enough to lean on if I need him.

"You *wanted* to adopt me?"

Matilda buries her face in Rick's chest and he nods soberly over her head. "Of course we did, son. We were there the day you were born and we loved you almost as much as your mother did. Then when she got sick, we promised her we'd take care of you if Gary couldn't. Raise you as our own."

Matilda steps out of his arms and wipes her cheeks, visibly trying to get herself together. "She was worried about leaving you with Gary, but she didn't want her parents anywhere near you. They weren't good people, she said. Rich but cruel. And once we started the adoption process after your father died, we found out she was right to worry."

As she continues to speak, I feel more and more like I've stepped into a badly written soap opera. But this is my actual life. Soap operas have to be based on some grain of truth, right? Well, maybe not.

According to Matilda my story seems to be about rich, entitled grandparents that didn't want the responsibility of taking care of me, but also were against losing their last surviving heir to someone whose blood was a little less blue. And they were willing to drag everyone involved into a long court battle because of it.

Talk about family values.

My foster mother, the brilliant lawyer, made a deal in order to stop that from happening and to keep me away from them. No legal adoption in return for no further contact or financial inducement. Instead, the inheritance that had been meant for my mother would be held in a trust for me until I hit the ripe old age of thirty.

Apparently it's a lot of money.

"That doesn't sound like that big of a deal," Royal says, arms crossed over his barrel chest. "Rich, evil grandparents and white boy problems. What was all the secrecy about?"

I turn toward him with wide eyes. "It doesn't sound like a big deal? I thought I was…that they had to take me because…"

Rick steps over to me, reaches down and pulls me up into his arms, holding me tight. "We were afraid we'd lose you. We thought you'd resent us and want to be with your real family."

I see Matilda standing stiffly to the side and I tug her close. Other than Royal, we've never been natural huggers, but damn it, it's time we learned. "You are my family. You've always been my family. I guess because of…where I came from, I didn't think I deserved to be yours."

"That might be the most preposterous thing you've ever said. And if we're family then it's time you acted like it." Matilda says all this as sharply as she can while pressed against my chest. "I'm talking regular phone calls and multiple holidays in person each year. And next time, we'll watch Leia's Wars together."

Star Wars. But I'm not correcting her.

"And we're getting you a new apartment," Rick grumbles. "In a better neighborhood with stronger locks. And a car."

Matilda lifts her head. "Unless you're choosing not to own one to have a smaller carbon footprint. Do you even have a driver's license?"

"Are we making demands now?" Royal jumps in, smiling at our awkward group hug. "Let's have him clean my apartment once a month for a year to make up for what he's done to it this week."

I move out of the embrace, smirking at my brother and take a warning step closer, making him laugh.

"Careful," he chuckles, holding up his hands to ward me off. "You need to stop randomly hitting people for no reason now that you're loaded. That's just asking for a lawsuit."

"I'm not loaded." I look over at Matilda. "I don't want or need anything from them. I have you."

She's smiling tearfully. "I'm so proud of you, JD."

Royal and I both gasp like dying fish and she shakes her head. "Stop it. We're not perfect. And Lauren wanted you to have that inheritance. You can give it to charity if you want, or start a nonprofit of your own, but in a few years, you're going to take it. If only to keep it out of their hands."

I can't win an argument with Matilda. It's never been done. "Yes, ma'am."

She takes my hand in both of hers and looks into my eyes. "Now about that friend of Ken's that Rick likes so much."

As fast as that, my mood crashes. "Don't start. I know I screwed things up with him. But… I think I love him." I glance over at Royal. "I know I do. You were right. I need to find a way to tell him. Convince him I deserve another chance."

Matilda walks back over to the file she'd set down on the table, opens it, and pulls out an envelope. "This might give you some ideas."

I'm almost afraid to take it. We've had a few too many revelations today. "What is it?"

"Ken said it's a letter from a man who reads your column. He needs some advice." Her wink startles me so much it takes me a minute to register what she's saying. "He calls himself Green's Marine."

CHAPTER ELEVEN

Sometimes all you want in life is to rewind the last two weeks and make a different decision, one that would guarantee you'd be cuddled up on the couch of the man you had a thing for, taking the occasional break to have hot, sweaty sex until you felt better about the world.

But time travel hasn't been invented yet, so you're going to have to do things the old fashioned way.

If you groveled, this would be the perfect time.

"You look like you might throw up, JD. Here. Drink this." Fiona pushes my favorite beer in my direction, leaning on the bar so she doesn't have to shout to be heard over the raucous crowd. "And stop worrying. Everything's going to be fine."

"Unless he doesn't show up."

"He will. Haven't you seen that Drew Barrymore movie? It'll be just like that. Only more X-rated."

I work up a weak glare at her words of comfort. She's not the first person in the last day or two to mention the fact that my big, brilliant idea is derivative of a romantic comedy about never being kissed.

I thought I'd been inspired after reading his letter. I wanted to give him the same honesty he'd given to me, only in public via my last Dry Spell Diary. No matter what happened tonight it would be my last. There was no point in looking for something else. Someone else, when I'd already had exactly what I wanted.

I'm not sure what he thought about it, but I have it on good authority he actually read it. It's clear from the crowd inside Finn's that a lot of people did.

My readers, at least, were on my side and all in. It had only been four days since the article went online, and some of them already made t-shirts.

Go Green, Marine.

The outpouring of support was unexpected, but welcome. The fact that Fiona and Wyatt had gotten a handful of the Finn family to show up as well—including the owner and his husband was…awkward, but also welcome.

I'm still not sure what Joey is doing here. He said something about expanding his company, but I get the feeling he drew the brotherly short straw since Royal had an overseas flight, and he's just here to keep an eye on me.

"Is it usually this crowded? You're a fireman, Finn. Isn't this some kind of health hazard or code violation?" Joey shakes his head of curly dark hair as he observes the crowd.

Wyatt, who's standing beside me and giving me an insane case of déjà vu says, "It's fine. Besides, it's a special occasion." He smirks at me, then tilts his head toward my brother. "So I hear you're a babysitter?"

The front door opens and half the bar turns toward the newcomer, who looks awkwardly around and shrugs before greeting his friends with a wave.

He's not coming. I stand up, sick to my stomach. "I'll be back."

Why did this ever sound romantic? I think as I make my way to the bathroom, nodding each time someone waves or calls my name. I hate being the center of attention. I'm a people watcher. Real or fictional, as long as none of those people are looking back at me, I'm good.

Unless it's Carter. I love the way he looks at me. *Looked* at me.

I walk into the empty employee restroom in the back—knowing Fiona has perks—and stare at my reflection over the sink. I think I look the same as I did three weeks ago, but everything has changed. I've changed.

That's why this has to work, because I'm not sure I can go back to the way life was before I knew him. I don't want to go back to that. Not when I know it can be so much more.

Not after he wrote that letter. If I hadn't already been in love with him, what he'd written would have sealed the deal for me.

God, that letter…

Dear Green,

I'm not sure how to start this. I've never asked for advice about romance before, unless you count my Gran. I once asked her how she knew she was in love with my grandfather and she told me, "He looked at me and I saw my future."

At the time, I'll admit it sounded vague and frankly unhelpful. Something people say when they aren't sure how to respond. And then one night I looked up and saw a beautiful man looking back at me. And I saw exactly what she'd been talking about. My future.

It surprised me, but I didn't question my good fortune. I knew he was too young, too smart and a little too stubborn not to be a challenge, but none of that mattered. He was my future, and knowing that, I expected everything else to fall into place.

But it didn't. Instead he shared some things with me that were personal and precious, and by the next morning, he was gone.

I've thought a lot about why, and I have to take responsibility for my part in things. I was going too fast. Pushing too hard. And he'd told me a story, but I didn't return the favor. If I could go back, that's what I would change.

I'd tell him about a man who'd served his country for his entire adult life. Proudly and gratefully, with no regrets save one. That he'd done all of it alone. He'd lived each day for his duty, and came home each night to no one.

He wasn't without camaraderie and friendship, loyalty and occasional intimacy, but there was no one that belonged to him. No one to share his successes and failures with, or tell his secrets to. No one to miss him when he was away.

And he'd gone to too many funerals. After a memorial for yet another life cut short in service, the man went directly to his commanding officer and resigned. He accepted a job from an old recruit and friend, bought a new truck and packed up his life. He left everything he knew behind. Not because life was too short. But because when you lived it alone, it was too damn long.

I suppose the reason I wrote to you for advice was to ask if that story would have made a difference. If the man I fell for would have understood why I was so thankful for running into him that night at the bar. And that even if nothing had happened to throw us together, I would have found a way to bring him home.

Signed, Green's Marine

I didn't share it online. I couldn't, it felt too personal. But I responded to it in my article. I also asked him to give me another chance to share the future he'd seen with me.

The men in North Carolina must be insane. I honestly don't know how someone so sexy and nurturing, vital and dynamic could have lived such a solitary life.

I guess we'd both lived alone for years. Despite the crowd around us.

But we'd seen each other. That had to mean something. It had to be big enough to overcome my bad decision-making.

It—

I heard the door close an instant before two large hands land on my shoulders. "There you are. What are you overthinking now, grasshopper?"

My knees collapse and I sag against him. "Carter."

He turns me around with a worried frown. "Jesus, I'm sorry, JD. I shouldn't have snuck up on you like that. Not here. I wasn't thinking."

"You're here."

He rubs his bearded jaw self-consciously. "Brady snuck me in the back way. There are a lot of curious people out there, but you were the only one I wanted to see."

"I didn't realize they'd… I wanted to do something big so you'd know."

His espresso eyes are warm as he studies my face. "So I'd know what? I think I got your message, but I needed to be sure you meant it. I needed to be looking at you."

I lick lips that are suddenly dry. "I've never been in love with anyone before, Zeus. You'll have to be patient with me, because this probably won't be the last time I screw things up. But even when I do, I promise I won't run away again."

There's no chance to say anything else because he's kissing me. His hands wrap around my biceps and he pulls me up against him, walking me backwards until my back is against the door.

This. Fucking. Kiss. I've missed it. Craved it. Woke up dreaming about the scrape of his beard and his full, soft lower lip.

Missed you so much.

"JD," he moans, his hands lowering to grab my ass and drag me closer. "Fuck, baby, I need to get you home. Now."

"You're always trying to take me home." But I can't wait that long. I pull a slim packet of lube out of my pocket and slip it into his hand. I'd been prepared. Just in case. "Right here."

"With all those people outside?" He swears and rocks his erection against mine. But he doesn't say no. "Condom?"

"We don't need one."

I kiss him again before he can ask another question, reaching between us to undo his jeans and mine. I need him. I need to feel him inside me again. To know he belongs to me.

"You're still working on deserving that spanking, aren't you, baby?" he mutters, turning me to face the door and dragging my pants to my knees.

God, yes. "Please, Carter. Do it. Fuck me. Love me."

"I do, baby. You know I do."

I hear the packet tear and then his wet fingers are massaging my needy hole.

"Damn it, I hope you're ready. Because I can't..." The head of his bare cock is pushing through the still-tight barrier and I cry out in breathless surprise. So full it's almost painful, but I'll kill him if he stops.

He freezes, letting us both enjoy the sensation of him inside me, his strong body curved around mine.

"Oh God," I moan and his hand covers my mouth to muffle the sound.

"I keep telling you this is for me and I don't want to share it." He's growling, tilting my hips with his free hand so he can get deeper. *God, so deep.*

"This is just for us," he says, grinding and pulsing

against me until I'm not-so-silently begging for more. He drops his forehead onto my back. "Baby, you feel so good with nothing between us. I've never done this without protection. It feels… I don't think I can go slow."

I'm his first.

I don't want it slow. I lick his palm, trying to tell him what I need and he groans, hips slinging against me in a way that makes us both gasp in pleasure.

Yes. Hard. Fuck me hard.

He has the same idea.

"Missed you," he moans, starting a fast, punishing rhythm. "So much, JD."

Don't stop.

There's no more hesitation. No going slow. He's fucking me so hard now the door I'm clinging to rattles with every thrust. I want it to last, but I'm desperate to come.

Carter mutters filthy things in my ear and his hand strokes my cock roughly, bringing me to the edge so we can fly off it together.

"When I get you home I'm taking my time with you," he swears softly. "I'll tie you to the bed if I have to, and you'll let me, won't you?"

Yes. I nod desperately.

"Fuck, I'm close. Come with me, JD. I need you to… I love you, baby."

Love you, Zeus.

My orgasm hits me hard, arching my back and nearly lifting me off the floor. I shout his name into his hand and shake against him.

Then Carter is joining me, filling me up with the hot pulsing jets of his release. Owning me. Marking me. "Yes, JD. *Fuck.*"

Love you.

When we're both steady enough to step away from the door, he turns me in his arms and kisses me with so much tenderness I nearly break.

"Did you know the first time I saw you I thought about bathroom sex? That I'd never done it before, but I'd be willing to give it a shot for Big Daddy Zeus?"

He lets out a surprised laugh. "Was it worth it?"

"Totally."

"Do you want to know what I thought about the first time I saw you?" he asks.

"I already do." I look up at him and smile. "I read your letter, remember?"

He holds me closer. "And I finally read your diary.

Every word."

"So now the only secret you're still keeping between us is the recipe for that delicious barbecue sauce."

"Every relationship needs a little mystery."

There's a loud knock on the door. "Guys?"

It's Fiona. And my pants are still clinging to my knees.

Shitballs.

"It's getting crazy out here, JD. If you're done pretending you're a kinky Finn, Green's Marine needs to make a quick appearance. I'm serious, you're on cleanup if they riot."

Carter looks at me and we both laugh. "We'll be there in a minute."

"And then you'll come home with me?"

I can read him now. Happy. In love. Still worried I might run away.

"And then we'll go home together."

Once you have found him, never let him go.

South Pacific again.

Sorry. Couldn't resist.

Short excerpt from The Dry Spell Diaries
by JD Green

Dear Diary,

This is the last time I'll be writing those words. Not because the dry spell is over, though it is. It really is. And not because my editor wants me to move on, because believe me, he really doesn't.

Want to know the reason? Come closer, dear readers, and I'll tell you my story. It starts with the worst date I've ever had, but it really takes off after that. The working title is Green's Marine, and I think you're going to love it as much as I do. As long as you can help me fix the ending.

Ready to hear the details?

One night at Finn's… Everything changed.

THANKS FOR READING!

I truly hope you enjoyed this book. If so, please leave a review and tell your friends. Word of mouth and online reviews are immensely helpful to authors and greatly appreciated.

To keep up with all the latest news about my books, release info, exclusive excerpts and more, check out my website **RGAlexander.com**, Friend me on **Facebook**, or follow me on **Twitter**.

If you love the ***Finn Factor*** series and want to hang out with like-minded others, as well as get access to exclusive discussions and enter the frequent ***contests*** and ***free book giveaways*** each month contests, join **The Finn Club** on Facebook:)

Friend me on **Facebook**
https://www.facebook.com/RGAlexander.RachelGrace
to join **THE FINN CLUB**
https://www.facebook.com/groups/911246345597953/
for contests, and smutty fun.

CHECK OUT Curious,
BOOK 1 OF THE FINN FACTOR SERIES

"Everyone go buy the f***ing thing. Curious. Go now." tweet
by author of Love Lessons,
Heidi Cullinan

*"When I got to the end of this book, I wanted to start over…
RG Alexander is one hell of an author!"*
USA Today bestselling **Bianca Sommerland**,
author of Iron Cross, the Dartmouth Cobras

Are you Curious?

Jeremy Porter is. Though the bisexual comic book artist
has known Owen Finn for most of his life—long enough

to know that he is terminally straight—he can't help but imagine what things would be like if he weren't.

Owen is far from vanilla—as a dominant in the local fetish community, he sees as much action as Jeremy does. Lately even more.

Since Jeremy isn't into collars and Owen isn't into men, it seems like his fantasies will remain just that forever…until one night when Owen gets curious.

Warning: **READ THIS!** Contains explicit m/m nookie. A lot of it. Very detailed. Two men getting kinky, talking dirty and doing the horizontal mambo. Are you reading this? Do you see them on the cover? Guy parts will touch. You have been warned.

Available Now!

Check out all the other books in the Finn Factor series.
www.RGAlexander.com

Big Bad John
Bigger in Texas series, Book One

Available Now!
www.RGAlexander.com

Kinda broad at the shoulder and narrow at the hip…

Trudy Adams never planned on going home again. Not to that sleepy little Texas town where everyone knew her business and thought she was trouble. She ran away to California years ago, and now, after what has felt like a lifetime of struggling, her lucky break might finally be around the corner.

And then she got that email.

John Brown has been waiting patiently for Trudy to return, but his patience has run out. He's had years to think about all the things he wants to do to her, and he's willing to use her concern for her brother, her desire to help her best friend get her story, and every kinky fantasy Trudy has to show her who she belongs to.

The explosive chemistry between them is unmistakable. But will history and geography be obstacles they can't overcome? When Trouble makes a two-week deal with Big Bad...anything can happen.

Warning: **READ THIS!** BDSM, explicit sex, voyeurism, accidental voyeurism, voyeurism OF voyeurism with a sprinkle of m/m, exhibitionism, ropes, cuffs, gratuitous spanking, skinny dipping, irresponsible use of pervertables...and a big, dirty man who will melt your heart.

BILLIONAIRE BACHELORS SERIES

Available Now!
www.RGAlexander.com

Glass slipper shopping can be a dangerous pastime…

The CEO's Fantasy-Book 1

Dean Warren is the billionaire CEO of Warren Industries. He's spent the last five years proving his worth and repairing his family's reputation. But the rules he's had to live by are starting to chafe, especially when it comes to one particular employee. He doesn't believe in coincidence, but when Sara Charles shows up suddenly unemployed and asking him to agree to a month of indulging their most forbidden fantasies--there's no way he can refuse.

When reality is better than his wildest dreams, will the CEO break all of his own rules to keep her?

The Cowboy's Kink-Book 2

Tracy Reyes is a man who enjoys having control. Over his family's billion dollar land and cattle empire, over the women he tops at the club, and over his life. When teacher Alicia Bell drops into his lap with a problem that needs solving and a body that begs to be bound, he can't resist the opportunity to give her the education in kink she needs. But can he walk away from his passionate pupil when it's time to meet his future bride?

The Playboy's Ménage-Book 3

Henry Vincent and Peter Faraday have been friends forever. The royal rocker and polymath playboy have more than a few things in common. They're both billionaires, they both love a challenge...and they've both carried a long-lasting torch for the woman that got away. Finding Holly again brings back feelings and memories neither one of them wanted to face. But they'll have to if they want to share her. Keeping her from running again and making her admit how she feels about them will take teamwork. Hours of teamwork...and handcuffs.

The Bachelors

We know every debutante's mama wants a piece of their action, but if you could choose without repercussions, which of the Billionaire Bachelors would be your fantasy? The true hardcore cowboy who has enough land and employees to start his own country, but no dancing partner for his special kind of two-step? The musician with a royal pedigree, a wild streak and a vast fortune at his disposal, who's never been seen with the same woman twice? His best jet-setting buddy who can claim no less than five estates, four degrees and three charges of lewd public behavior on his record? Or the sweet-talking, picture-perfect tycoon-cum-philanthropist who used to be the baddest of the bunch but put those days behind him when he took over as CEO of his family's company? (Or did he?)

Pick your fantasy lover--rocker, rancher, rebel or reformed rogue. Glass slipper shopping is a dangerous sport to be sure, especially with prey as slippery as these particular animals, but I'll still wish all my readers happy hunting.

From Ms. Anonymous
Available Now!
www.RGAlexander.com

OTHER BOOKS FROM R.G. ALEXANDER

<u>Fireborne Series</u>
Burn With Me
Make Me Burn
Burn Me Down-*coming soon*

<u>Bigger in Texas Series</u>
Big Bad John
Mr. Big Stuff-
Big Trouble-*coming soon*

<u>The Finn Factor Series</u>
Curious
Scandalous
Dangerous
Ravenous
Finn Again
Shameless
Fearless
Lawless

<u>Billionaire Bachelors Series</u>
The CEO's Fantasy
The Cowboy's Kink
The Playboy's Ménage

<u>Children Of The Goddess Series</u>
Regina In The Sun
Lux In Shadow
Twilight Guardian
Midnight Falls

<u>Wicked Series</u>
Wicked Sexy
Wicked Bad
Wicked Release

Shifting Reality Series
My Shifter Showmance
My Demon Saint
My Vampire Idol

Temptation Unveiled Series
Lifting The Veil
Piercing The Veil
Behind The Veil

Superhero Series
Who Wants To Date A Superhero?
Who Needs Another Superhero?

Kinky Oz Series
Not In Kansas
Surrender Dorothy

Mènage and More
Truly Scrumptious
Three For Me?
Four For Christmas
Dirty Delilah
Marley in Chains

Anthologies
Three Sinful Wishes
Wasteland - Priestess
Who Loves A Superhero?

Bone Daddy Series
Possess Me
Tempt Me
To The Bone

Elemental Steam Series Written As Rachel Grace
Geared For Pleasure

ABOUT R.G. ALEXANDER

R.G. Alexander is a *New York Times* and *USA Today* Bestselling author who has written over 40 erotic paranormal, contemporary, sci-fi/fantasy books for multiple e-publishers and Berkley Heat.

She has lived all over the United States, studied archaeology and mythology, been a nurse, a vocalist, and now a writer who dreams of vampires, witches and airship battles. RG feels lucky every day that she gets to share her stories with her readers, and she loves talking to them on Twitter and FB. She is happily married to a man known affectionately as The Cookie—her best friend, research assistant, and the love of her life. Together they battle to tame the wild Rouxgaroux that has taken over their home.

To Contact R. G. Alexander:
www.RGAlexander.com
Facebook:
http://www.facebook.com/RachelGrace.RGAlexander
Twitter: https://twitter.com/RG_Alexander

Made in the USA
Columbia, SC
09 July 2020